The Treasure Is
Love

The Treasure Is Love

Barbara Cartland

THORNDIKE
CHIVERS

This Large Print edition is published by Thorndike Press®, Waterville, Maine USA and by BBC Audiobooks Ltd, Bath, England.

Published in 2005 in the U.S. by arrangement with Cartland Promotions.

Published in 2006 in the U.K. by arrangement with Cartland Promotions, c/o Rupert Crew Limited.

U.S. Hardcover 0-7862-8142-1 (Romance)
U.K. Hardcover 1-4056-3607-6 (Chivers Large Print)

The text of this Large Print edition is unabridged.
Other aspects of the book may vary from the original edition.

Set in 16 pt. Plantin by Al Chase.

Printed in the United States on permanent paper.

British Library Cataloguing-in-Publication Data available

Library of Congress Cataloging-in-Publication Data

Cartland, Barbara, 1902–
    The treasure is love / by Barbara Cartland.— Large print ed.
    p. cm. — (Thorndike Press large print romance)
    Originally published: Arrow Books, 1979.
    ISBN 0-7862-8142-1 (lg. print : hc : alk. paper)
    1. Napoleonic Wars, 1800–1815 — Veterans — Fiction.
    2. Administration of estates — Fiction.   3. Disinheritance —
    Fiction.   4. Large type books.   I. Title.   II. Thorndike
    Press large print romance series.
    PR6005.A765T74 2005
    823′.912—dc22   2005022115

The Treasure Is
Love

Author's Note

On August 11th, 1815, two months after Waterloo, the Prime Minister warned the country that the financial situation was very grave.

The Navy and Army were the first to be pared. Within eighteen months 300,000 soldiers and sailors were turned adrift.

The men who had fought their way from Torres Vedras to Toulouse were given neither pension nor medal. The finest Army England had ever had was dismissed without regret or gratitude.

Chapter 1

1816

The man astride a magnificent black stallion rode down the overgrown drive avoiding a number of dead branches which had fallen from the oak trees which bordered it.

He crossed the stone bridge which spanned the lake and rode into the court-yard where the gravel was almost obscured by moss and weeds.

He pulled his horse to a standstill and sat looking up at the huge stone crest which surmounted the ancient door.

For some moments he stared at it as if looking back into the history of those to whom it had belonged.

Then his eyes moved to notice the number of diamond-paned windows that had lost their glass, the bricks which needed pointing, the stone ornamentation which was chipped or broken.

Slowly turning his head upwards, he saw the balustrade which bordered the roof was missing in a number of places.

He sighed and, dismounting, patted his horse on the neck saying:

"Go and find some grass, Salamanca, but do not go too far."

The horse appeared to understand what was said to him and moved across the courtyard towards the high grass which covered what had once been a smooth lawn.

His owner watched him go. Then, as if he knew it was hopeless to try to enter the house through the front door, he walked round the side of the building which led directly ahead to the stables and on the left to the tradesmen's entrance.

This he saw was overgrown with laurels and other shrubs which, in the old days, had been kept tidy and under control.

There was no sign of any life and at first he thought the house was deserted. Then rounding the shrubs he saw the back door was ajar and walked in.

In front of him was a long flagged passage with a dairy opening off it, on his right.

He glanced in and saw that the marble slabs which had once held huge bowls of cream were empty and walked on until he came first to the scullery, then to the huge high-ceilinged kitchen.

He remembered it when the beams were

hung with hams and the range was covered with a dozen brass pots and pans.

Mrs Briggs, who had cooked for his father and was known for the excellence of her roasts, would be busy at the spotlessly scrubbed kitchen-table with at least three kitchen-maids and several scullions to wait on her.

Now he thought the great kitchen would be empty just as the dairy had been. Then he saw sitting in a corner a little white-haired woman shelling some peas from their pods into a bowl which she held on her lap.

For a moment he stared at her incredulously and then as she looked up at him, he moved forward to say:

"Mrs Briggs! It is Mrs Briggs?"

The old woman looked at him through eyes which found it difficult to focus. Then she exclaimed:

"Master Tyson! I'd have known your voice anywhere!"

She tried to get up, but Tyson Dale moved forward to put a hand on her shoulder and say:

"No, do not move. It is nice to see you again. I was half-afraid you would not be here."

"Oh, I be here, Master Tyson, an' you're

a sight for sore eyes after so many years away!"

"Thirteen to be exact!" Tyson Dale said.

He pulled up a kitchen-chair and sat down beside her, thinking as he did so that Mrs Briggs must be well into her eighties, for she had been an old woman when he had left England for India thirteen years ago in 1803.

"How've you been keeping, Master Tyson?" Mrs Briggs asked conversationally.

"Well enough," Tyson Dale replied, "but now the war is over and the Army has no further use for soldiers I have come home."

Mrs Briggs looked startled.

"You don't intend to live here, Master Tyson?"

"I have nowhere else to go."

Mrs Briggs shook her head.

"It won't be very comfortable for you. Briggs and I've done our best, but a big house like this is too much for two old people."

"You have no-one to help you?"

"There were no money to pay anyone after your father died, Master Tyson. But Briggs and I stayed on because we'd no-where else to go."

Tyson Dale's lips tightened.

"What happened to my father's money?

He must have left some!"

"How should we know, Master Tyson?" Mrs Briggs asked. "All we was told was that the house was yours if you ever returned from that terrible war, and after that no-one has come near us."

"How have you managed?" Tyson Dale enquired.

"We had a little put by, Briggs and me, but it weren't much, and this last year we've found it hard to make ends meet."

Tyson Dale put his hand into his pocket.

"I will try to make it up to you," he said, "but I will be frank and tell you it is not going to be easy. But here at least are some sovereigns to be going on with. Perhaps you will manage some sort of meal for me to-night."

Mrs Briggs looked at the golden sovereigns incredulously as if she could hardly believe they were real.

Then as her hand closed over them she said:

"I'll be making up your father's room for you. That's where you'll sleep now you are the Master, and thank goodness there's nothing wrong with the ceiling!"

Tyson Dale was just about to ask her what she meant by that when he realised the answer.

Of course, with the house left to decay and no repairs being done for so long, it was inevitable that the ceilings would fall with the damp. Without even asking he was sure that the top floor would be uninhabitable.

As he left the kitchen he noticed there was dust and cobwebs everywhere and he knew there was nobody to blame but himself, but as it happened there was nothing he could have done about it.

He had returned from India and had been fighting with Wellington's Army in Portugal when the letter which had taken a long time to reach him, informed him of his father's death.

It was not until a year later that he learnt that as the Solicitors had found it impossible to find any documents confirming his father's marriage, his uncle had claimed the position of heir presumptive to his grandfather, Lord Wellingdale.

A year later he learnt by chance through a belated copy of *The Morning Post* that his grandfather was dead, and his uncle, his father's younger brother, had become the 6th Lord Wellingdale.

At the time, it did not seem to Tyson Dale of any particular importance. He had been too concerned, as were those with whom he served, with fighting Napoleon. England

and the problems of social life there seemed very small and far away.

It was only now when he had returned to an island triumphant at having beaten the greatest tyrant Europe had ever known that he began to ask himself what would happen to him in the future.

It seemed incredible that Britain had defeated, contrary to all expectations, a martial state with a population at the start of the war nearly three times the size of her own.

With most of Europe mobilised against what Napoleon had called contemptuously 'a nation of shop-keepers' they had conquered utterly destroying him and his power.

Tyson Dale knew that for all the island's sacrifices, he had, during the twenty-two years' struggle, grown richer than ever before.

But while communications, merchant tonnage, conquests all over the world had created for England a rich, prosperous Empire, Tyson Dale had to face the fact that like a great number of those who were responsible for the victory, he was penniless.

As usually happened after a war, the men who had been acclaimed heroes while they were fighting were now thrown back into civilian life, the majority of them without pensions.

There was no recompense, not only for having risked their lives in the struggle but the loss of their jobs, their savings and in many cases their wives, their homes and their families.

Tyson Dale at least had no-one to worry about except himself.

At the same time he had wondered ever since he had landed at Dover with his total possessions consisting of his uniform and his charger, Salamanca, what he was to do.

'At least,' he thought, 'I have Revel Royal.'

"Revel Royal!" he exclaimed bitterly beneath his breath, as he walked along the corridor. There was nothing Royal about it now!

The house had been left to his father not by the Dales who would have undoubtedly claimed it as they had claimed the title, estate and his grandfather's fortune, but by his father's mother who had been an Osborne.

Because she wanted to feel that her eldest son, Hubert, was independent of his father, she had made over the house she had inherited to him, but unfortunately had not been allowed to allot any of the money with the gift.

Tyson Dale, however, knew that his father when he was a young man had had an allowance from his father which he was clever enough, in one way or another, to make into a small fortune so that he could do as he wished.

To his family's fury, instead of marrying the girl they had chosen for him, he ran away with the pretty daughter of the local Vicar when she was still young enough to require her father's permission to marry.

As this was not forthcoming because Lord Wellingdale owned the living of which her father was the incumbent, Hubert Dale and Mary Dawson just disappeared.

Despite the extensive search that was made for them because Lord Wellingdale was angry and by the Reverend Dawson because he was told to, they did not reappear until Mary was over twenty-one.

Then they went to Revel Royal and lived there, announcing that they were man and wife and had a two-year-old son called Tyson.

Lord Wellingdale was not interested.

He was an obstinate, self-opinioned man who disliked opposition of any sort and expected his sons to obey him as if they were soldiers under his command.

His second son George was far more pliable and thought that if his elder brother Hubert was such a fool as to give up all the comforts that were to be found at home and to ignore the social advantages of taking a wife who would be accepted by the King and Queen and those who circled round the court in London, that was his look-out.

George married a woman of whom his father greatly approved and who was a titled heiress in her own right.

Lady Edith Dale had no wish to seek out the acquaintance of a Parson's daughter, even if she was her sister-in-law, and George had always been jealous of his elder brother.

Tyson could never remember either his uncle, his aunt, or his grandfather for that matter, ever coming to Revel Royal, and if his father spoke of his relations, it was with a mocking bitterness.

His mother, however, had been very content to be without them.

She loved the man with whom she had run away with an unswerving devotion that made life at Revel Royal a happy one, not only for her husband, but also for her son.

Looking back although he was only a child, Tyson could never remember feeling lonely or missing the companionship of other children.

There had been so many things for him to do — horses to ride, game to shoot, fishing in the lake, trees to climb, and a father who wished to share with him all the problems and triumphs of a small agricultural estate.

And yet, he thought, as he went into the Library where he had so often sat with his father when he was a boy, talking over the plans of what they could do if they could afford it and if next year's harvest was a good one, the mere fact that his world had been so small had made him adventurous.

He joined the Army because he wanted to enlarge his horizons and he had been an exceptional soldier because he had known how to handle men.

He had talked to those who served under him as his father had talked to his employees and they followed him and were ready to fight or die with him.

He thought when he first heard of his father's death and that his uncle had made himself accepted as heir presumptive to the title, that it would be quite easy when he returned home to prove that his father and mother were married.

In which case he himself would be the

right and proper successor to his grand-father.

It was impossible for him to return to England to see to what seemed a very trivial personal matter compared to the defeat of Napoleon Bonaparte, but he wrote to his father's Solicitor, a man he had known all his life.

He told him to find the necessary particulars of the marriage and to ask his mother where the ceremony had taken place.

It was some months later before he learnt that his letter had arrived after his mother had also died and although a thorough search had been made at Revel Royal there were no documents to show that a marriage had taken place, or that he, Tyson, had been born in wedlock.

Tyson Dale thought the whole situation was ridiculous and he had not realised how serious it was until a newspaper told him that his uncle had become the 6th Lord Wellingdale.

This entitled his cousin Manfred, whom he had always disliked, to become the Honourable, while Tyson himself dared not assume that even the name of Dale was his legally.

'I will sort it all out when I get home,' he had thought optimistically.

But now, looking at the dilapidation all round him, he knew that to fight such a case would cost money.

If he was to feed himself in the meantime he could not afford a Solicitor's fees.

The Library seemed smaller than he remembered it, but it was still a very beautiful room.

The bright leather covers of the books had long ago faded and become grey with dust. Dust obscured the colours on the painted ceiling and there were so many panes of broken glass stuffed with rags that when he drew back the tattered and frayed curtains the light seemed to percolate only fitfully.

It was ten years since his father had died and a great deal could have happened in that time.

Upstairs the house was very much as he might have expected.

The huge four-poster beds were unchanged. They had been at Revel Royal, so legend said, since the house had obtained its name from Charles II who had stayed there for a riotous weekend surrounded by the beautiful women who amused him.

He had told his host, Sir Thomas Osborne, before he left that because he had enjoyed himself so immensely, the house was to be known in the future as 'Revel Royal'.

Its shabby and threadbare appearance now was merely a mockery of the grandeur and glamour which it had once had.

Tyson Dale walked on, hearing loose floorboards crack beneath his feet, seeing everywhere fallen plaster or tattered wall-paper, finding as he had expected that the ceilings on the top floor lay on the ground.

The passages were almost impassable and as he descended the staircase from which a number of carved newel-posts seemed to have fallen or been lost he wondered once again what he could do about the house and about himself.

The Army had taught him self-assurance. It was impossible to command a number of men without assuming an authority which very quickly becomes habitual.

Now for the first time for many years Tyson Dale felt uncertain and insecure and these were sensations he did not enjoy.

The shadows were beginning to grow longer outside and old Briggs who had been his father's butler came shuffling into the Salon which seemed to be more faded and perhaps more empty than any other room in the house.

It was where his mother had always sat, and Tyson could remember when he was very young running excitedly down the stairs ahead of his Nurse because it was time for his mother to play with him and she would be waiting for him in the Salon.

The windows overlooked the rose-garden which had been her special delight, the sun-dial carrying the inscription that he had learned laboriously to read when he was quite small:

"Gather ye rosebuds while ye may, Old Time is still a-flying."

That was true enough, he thought now, and he wondered if there were other rose-buds he might have gathered when he was young, although many of them lingered in his memory and nothing could ever take these from him.

Always when he had been bivouacking on some hard exposed ground or billeted in some dirty and noisy Portuguese house that smelt abominably and was infested with fleas, his mind had returned to Revel Royal.

He had found himself transported as it were into a world he had loved as a child and in which he forgot the war and all the dis-comforts of it.

Instead he would remember all so clearly the first partridge he had shot and which he had carried proudly into the kitchen to show Mrs Briggs.

"I'll cook it for your supper, Master

Tyson," she had said.

"No," he answered. "It is for Mama, but I expect she will give me a taste of it."

"I'm sure she will," Mrs Briggs had replied, "and proud she'll be to know that you'll be as good a game-shot as your father."

There had been memories of the hay-fields when he had played among the stacks.

Memories too when everything had been white with snow and the Estate carpenter had made him a small toboggan on which he would ride triumphantly down the slopes invariably to overturn at the bottom.

There were so many memories, and always he had believed that when the war was over he would come back to Revel Royal and find it as he had left it.

"Where do I start?" he asked himself now, and heard old Briggs say:

"Your dinner's ready, Sir."

As soon as he turned the old man added in a very different tone of voice:

"It's real good to see you back, Master Tyson."

Briggs looked even older than his wife, but Tyson remembered they were in fact the same age.

He too had grown very thin and some-where he had found his ancient liveried coat and donned it.

It hung loosely on him, but to Tyson it was a gesture of welcome that warmed his heart and for the moment swept away the darkness and uncertainty of his thoughts.

He held out his hand.

"It is like home to find you and Mrs Briggs here. It would not be the same without you."

"Things aren't what they used to be, Master Tyson, but perhaps you'll be able to put 'em right again."

"I shall try," Tyson Dale replied, but he knew it was a hollow promise.

He needed money, but where was it to come from?

He ate the simple meal that Mrs Briggs cooked for him and waved aside the apologies of old Briggs that they would do better when he gave them more time.

"Tomorrow," Tyson said to himself, "I will shoot something for the pot and that at least will not cost anything."

Then he wondered if there were any cartridges for the guns which he had seen hanging as they had always done in the Gun-Room, and whether in fact there was anything to shoot.

There was so much he did not know, so much to discover about his home, and he was, although he would not admit it, afraid of what he might learn.

"I should have come back when Father died," he told himself when he had finished the simple meal.

"Is the *Dog and Duck* still there?" he asked aloud.

" 'Deed it is, Sir," Briggs replied, "but it's changed hands. Mr Tug died five years ago and a man called Finch 'as it now."

"I will go and call on him," Tyson said with a smile, "and I shall not be late. Do not wait up. Leave the front door open."

"I'll do that, Sir," Briggs said, "and perhaps you'd push the bolt in when you comes back. The lock's been broken for some years."

"I shall have to see about doing some repairs," Tyson replied.

He walked out of the Dining-Room where his meal had been served and along the corridor which led to the Hall.

There were a number of his grandmother's ancestors to stare at him from their gilt frames.

He had never thought them a particularly handsome lot, but he suddenly felt a surge of anger to think that the portraits of the Dales, a number of which had been painted by great Masters of Art, were now in the possession of his uncle.

"Dammit!" he told himself. "I will find some way to fight for my rights even if it takes me my whole lifetime!"

He walked out of the front door as he spoke and slammed it behind him because he was angry.

As he did so he wondered apprehensively if it might fall off its hinges and that too would need to be repaired.

He walked down the steps where there were weeds and a few brightly coloured flowers peeping from between the cracks in the stones and he whistled to Salamanca.

As if he remembered his orders the horse had not gone far and now he came trotting towards his master and started to nuzzle him.

Tyson Dale patted him on the neck.

"Had a good time, old boy?" he enquired. "Well, that is more than I have! When we come back we shall have to look at the stables and see what sort of state they are in to house you."

Salamanca nuzzled again as if he understood everything that was being said, then they trotted away down the drive towards the village.

It was a relief to find the black and white thatched cottages still looking much the same as they always had, the grey Norman

Church still standing, and the row of Alms Houses which his father had built unchanged.

He had the idea there were tiles missing and that doors and window-frames needed painting, but he did not want to look too closely and he rode on to the village green.

That at least was just as he remembered it.

The duck-pond in the centre, the ancient stocks which had not been used for a hundred years, and on the other side of it the *Dog and Duck* with its seat outside where the older members of the village would sit gossiping for hour after hour.

It was too late for the old cronies to be outside now, but Tyson could hear voices and laughter coming through an open window and thought that the Bar might be filled with old friends.

Then as he rode through the gateway at the side of the *Dog and Duck* where he knew he would find a small but adequate stable to leave Salamanca in, he drew in his breath in surprise.

Here things had certainly changed since he went away.

Now he could see the *Dog and Duck* had been extended at the back and the simple old village Public House had been turned into a Posting Inn.

The two-storey building must certainly, Tyson thought, contain a number of bed-rooms and on the other side of the court-yard there were new stables.

In case he had been mistaken in what he surmised, there were several vehicles in the centre of the yard to assure him his assump-tion was right.

The ostlers, if there were any, were obvi-ously too busy to attend to him, and Tyson found an empty stable and placed Salamanca inside it.

There was a manger with fresh hay and a few oats left by some rich man's horse which was not hungry and a bucket of water.

Tyson heard the noise of horses in the other stalls and when he walked across the courtyard and through the side door of the Inn towards the Bar, he thought it unlikely, from what he had just seen, that he would find any of the old villagers whom he had known as a child.

Several hours later Tyson realised that while he talked to a number of people and drank the best part of an excellent bottle of claret, he had not found any of his child-hood friends nor anyone to welcome him home as he had hoped they would.

The new Proprietor of the *Dog and Duck*

29

Mr Finch was different from Mr Tug who had been not only the village Inn-Keeper but also the village gossip.

There was nothing that went on that old Tug did not know and was prepared to chat about and speculate over for hours on end.

Finch, on the other hand, served Tyson Dale without showing any interest in his appearance, treating him only as a customer who might spend money.

Because he was lonely and because he wanted to talk to somebody — anyone would do — Tyson Dale got into conversation with some men who were on their way to the Races and to two others who had just returned from a Prize-Fight at which they had won a large sum of money.

He found himself accepting drinks he did not need since he preferred the claret which was of quite exceptional quality and which he suspected had been smuggled across the Channel.

Finally, as the Bar emptied and a number of those who had been drinking went up the stairs to bed, Tyson Dale told himself it was time he returned home.

He thought now he was less engaged that he might tell the Proprietor who he was, then decided against it.

He would perhaps come in another day

when the *Dog and Duck* was not so busy.

Besides he felt tired and the urge for conversation was over.

He paid what he owed and walked out into the courtyard.

As he did so he thought that after a long day in the saddle followed by a very small dinner he had had quite enough to drink.

Tyson Dale was usually very abstemious.

He had drunk the raw wines of Portugal and Spain mostly because they were safer than drinking water, and he had enjoyed the wines of France.

He liked to have a clear head in the morning. He only felt contempt for the notorious drunkenness of those who surrounded the Regent, who in his youth had been depicted often enough in the cartoons as being habitually drunk.

"I will be sober enough by the time I have ridden home on Salamanca," Tyson told himself.

He opened the door of the stable and as he did so Salamanca turned his head.

Tyson was just about to say, "I hope you had a good meal, old boy, for it is doubtful where your next one will come from!" when he heard a Gentleman's voice in the next stall ask:

"Have you given those coachmen enough

31

to keep them quiet for the next few hours?"

Tyson thought this was a strange question and listened for the answer.

It came from a man who was obviously uneducated.

"Don't ye worry, Guv'nor, they'll sleep loik logs 'til mornin' and wake wiv 'eads that'll make 'em wonder what 'it 'em!"

"That is good!" the Gentleman replied, "and I have doped the wine of the old couple. We will not hear from them either."

There was laughter at this and Tyson Dale gathered there were three men in the next stall.

The third man spoke.

"Wot'll we do now, Guv'nor?"

"You are coming with me, Jake," the Gentleman replied, "to bring down the young Lady's luggage while Bill puts the horses between the shafts. Mind you leave nothing behind. I am taking everything I can get!"

"Oi'll see ter that," Jake replied.

"Then follow me," the Gentleman said, "and get on with it, Bill. As soon as I bring the young Lady down we have to get out of here as quickly as possible."

"Yus, o' course, Sir Neville," Bill replied.

There was the sound of the two men's footsteps walking away followed by that of the horses being led into the yard.

Taking his hand from Salamanca's bridle Tyson Dale walked to the door which he had left half-open.

A man was leading horses already wearing their harnesses towards a closed travelling-carriage which was standing in the centre of the yard.

It was none of his business, Tyson Dale told himself.

At the same time he did not like the idea of coachmen and elderly people being drugged.

Then the frown between his eyes cleared and he told himself that what he had over-heard concerned a plan for the girl in ques-tion to elope with the Gentleman who had made the preparations.

It was all very romantic, and yet he found himself remembering how the Gentleman had said: "Mind you leave nothing behind. I am taking everything I can get!"

That sort of sentence did not seem very lover-like.

But perhaps young people had altered since he was last in England and he told himself once again that it was none of his business.

Then irresistibly because he was intrigued he walked across the yard and in through the side door which he knew the Gentleman and Jake had used.

After all there was no harm in seeing what was going on, and certainly the quiet village which had never known a scandal when he was a boy had changed in the years he had been away.

He walked slowly and deliberately and he knew without looking at him directly that Bill never even glanced in his direction as he secured the shafts to the horses' sides.

They looked good animals, capable, Tyson thought, of speed, and he was sure that the eloping couple would find no difficulty in out-running those who might pursue them.

He entered the new part of the building and saw that it had been planned spaciously with private Dining-Rooms opening off a fairly wide passage and a carpeted staircase to the floor above.

There was no sign of anyone on the Ground Floor and very quietly Tyson went up the stairs.

He had just reached the top when he saw a man coming towards him with a large trunk on his back.

Hastily he moved into the shadows and Jake, for it could be no-one else, passed without seeing him to descend the stairs cautiously.

Tyson moved on down the corridor.

Now he saw the light through the open door and paused as he drew nearer to it.

"Come on — hurry up!" he heard the Gentleman's voice say impatiently.

"H–how can I . . . dress with you . . . watching me?" a woman asked plaintively.

"I told you I have my eyes shut," the Gentleman answered, "and if you do not do as I say I will take you just as you are, and you will have to make the best of it!"

"You . . . dare not! I will not . . . let you! How can you . . . behave in this . . . outrageous manner?"

"I have told you that I intend to marry you — what more can you want?"

"I will not . . . marry you! You know I do not . . . love you!"

"I will make you a damned good husband, and you should be thankful for that."

"I have . . . no wish to . . . marry . . . anybody!" the girl replied and now Tyson could hear there were tears in her voice.

"Hurry up!" the Gentleman snapped, "and stop talking. I swear I will not wait much longer!"

The girl gave a little cry that was more like that of an animal in pain and Tyson felt himself involuntarily clenching his fists.

Then he had a sudden idea.

He moved swiftly back down the passage

and even as he did so realised that Jake was at the bottom of the staircase.

He only just had time to hide in the shadows as he had done before, when Jake passed him.

There was a murmur of voices and a minute or so later the man reappeared, this time with another large piece of luggage on his back and a smaller case in his hands.

He walked down the stairs and out into the courtyard.

Tyson followed him and watched him as he put the luggage down beside the carriage.

"There's one more," he said to Bill and turned to go back to the Inn.

Tyson waited in the passage and as Jake stepped in through the door and made towards the stairs he caught him with an uppercut on the chin that laid him out with hardly a murmur.

He was a large, rough man taken by surprise and he went down like a felled oak.

Tyson opened the door of the nearest room. It was a small private Dining-Room where the Gentry always preferred to eat alone if they were obliged to stop at a Posting Inn.

He pulled Jake inside, shut the door and locked it and walked up the stairs again.

He moved swiftly down the passage and

now he heard the girl's voice say:

"I must . . . get my shawl. I will be . . . cold without it."

"I will keep you warm in my arms!"

There was something mocking and unpleasant in the way the Gentleman spoke and it strengthened Tyson's grip as he seized him by the back of the neck.

He gave a gasp and tried to turn round to face his assailant, but it was impossible for him to do so.

He attempted to use his fists, but Tyson struck him as he had done his servant with a blow that lifted him off his feet! He fell with a crash, hitting his head as he did so against a corner of the chest-of-drawers.

He lay there completely unconscious with his legs sprawling out in front of him.

Tyson could see he was a very elegant-looking villain dressed in the height of fashion with a skilfully tied cravat which might easily have been the envy of the Dandy Set.

There was a little cry from behind him and Tyson turned from his contemplation of the man he had felled.

"You have . . . saved me! Who are . . . you? How could you have . . . come to my rescue at . . . exactly the right . . . moment?"

The words seemed to tumble over themselves and he saw that they came from a pair of very lovely curved lips in a small oval face with huge eyes which were raised to his.

As Tyson stared at her, thinking she was, in fact, the prettiest creature he had seen for a long time, the girl clasped her hands together.

"How can I . . . thank you?" she asked. "And . . . please . . . take me away from . . . here."

"Take you away?" Tyson enquired. "An elderly couple who I suspect are your Guardians have been drugged by this unpleasant Buck. But I am sure they will be all right in the morning and you will be able to continue your journey."

The girl glanced over her shoulder as if she half-expected to see the couple in question behind her. Then she said:

"Y–you . . . do not . . . understand."

"I am afraid not," Tyson said with a smile. "All I overheard was that this Gentleman's coachman had had orders to drug yours and this despicable creature lying at our feet doped the wine of those who are accompanying you."

He saw she was listening to him wide-eyed and added:

"I thought at first you were a pair of eloping lovers."

The girl shuddered.

"That is what he . . . wanted me to . . . be and because I . . . refused to . . . marry him he took . . . matters into his own . . . hands."

It struck Tyson that it was not surprising that anyone would want to marry anything so lovely.

She wore no bonnet, her fair hair, that in the candlelight held touches of red in it, framed her face and she was so small and yet so exquisitely made that it was hard to believe she was old enough to be married.

But when he looked at her figure and saw the blue silk travelling gown in the latest mode, there was no mistaking the curves of her breasts and the exquisite outline of her hips.

"Sir Neville was very . . . persistent," the girl said. "He would not take . . . no for an answer . . . but perhaps even he would be better than the . . . fate that awaits me if you will not . . . give me your . . . help."

"As I have already said, I do not understand," Tyson replied, "but having helped you so far I am quite prepared to do a little more if it is possible."

"Oh . . . thank you . . . thank you!" the girl cried. "I can see you are . . . kind . . . I know I can . . . trust you."

"Why should you be sure of that?" Tyson asked.

She made a little gesture with her hands.

"I . . . I do not . . . know . . . but I do . . . and you have come to my rescue when I thought I was completely and utterly lost . . . and I would have to do what Sir Neville wanted . . . or he threatened . . ."

She blushed and looked confused.

"I heard what he threatened," Tyson Dale said grimly. "Forget him!"

The girl glanced at the fallen figure apprehensively.

"S–suppose he . . . wakes up and . . . attacks you?"

"I think he is what they call 'out for the count'," Tyson said reassuringly.

"Please . . . take me somewhere safe . . . somewhere where I can . . . hide."

"Why should you want to do that?"

"Because my uncle and aunt are taking me to . . . London where I have to . . . marry a man I . . . l–loathe and . . . detest!"

"And you have to do as they say?"

"They are my Guardians . . . and I am only nineteen."

He had forgotten, Tyson thought, that young women under the age of twenty-one, and often older, were completely under the jurisdiction of their Guardian, whether he was a father or an uncle.

He thought it was unlikely that this small creature would be able to defy anyone in anything they intended her to do.

"I . . . I thought perhaps I could . . . kill myself . . . rather than marry someone I detest," the girl said in a very small voice, "but I did not . . . know how to go about it. It would be . . . awful if the gun misfired . . . or the knife only . . . w–wounded me!"

"You are not to talk like that!" Tyson said sharply. "You are young and you are lovely, and there must be somebody you wish to marry instead of someone you dislike!"

"I have never been allowed to . . . meet many gentlemen . . . only those of whom my uncle approved," she replied. "He sent Sir Neville away . . . and now you see the result."

"All men are not so unpleasant," Tyson assured her, "and perhaps when your uncle recovers from the doped wine you can talk to him and make him see sense where you are concerned."

"Never . . . never!" she cried. "He has made up his mind that I shall . . . marry this . . . gentleman whom we are to meet in London . . . and my aunt . . . who dislikes me . . . agrees it is the . . . right thing for me to do."

Tyson stood looking at the pleading eyes raised to his.

He told himself that if he had any sense he had done enough. He had saved this girl, who was little more than a child, from being abducted.

Now he should fade out of the picture and leave her future to take care of itself.

As if she knew the indecision going on within his mind, she said more insistently:

"Please . . . please . . . you are my only . . . hope. If you fail me . . . I really will . . . k–kill myself! I cannot do what they want . . . I cannot!"

"Why?" Tyson asked bluntly.

"Because if this . . . man they want me to marry even . . . touches my hand . . . it makes me creep . . . there is something . . . wrong . . . wicked, I think . . . about him. I know it in my heart . . . but when I tried to explain . . . they just said it was my imagination."

Tyson was silent and she moved a little nearer to him.

"If you could just . . . hide me for a day or two . . . while I think what I can do . . . while I try to remember if there is anyone who would be kind to me, and I will thank you . . . all the days of my life from the bottom of my . . . heart!"

She looked up at him. Then she said:

"If you refuse . . . then I must try to go away . . . alone. Do you think I would be able to hire a carriage here to carry me to London?"

"You cannot go to London alone," Tyson said.

"Then perhaps there is . . . somewhere else? Dover is not far from here."

Tyson thought of Dover as he had seen it that morning filled with soldiers pouring across the Channel — men roaming the streets, drunk and excited at their new-found liberty.

Officers in the Lord Warden Hotel had been toasting victory with any sort of wine they could afford to buy.

"You cannot go to Dover," he said sharply.

"There must be other . . . places," the girl said despairingly.

"Now just consider for a moment," Tyson said. "You are obviously used to living in luxury and comfort and having everything you want. You may be forced into a marriage which seems unpleasant, but women learn to make the best of things and perhaps when you get to know this man better, you will love him."

"Never! Never!" she replied. "I have told

you that he . . . disgusts me! I would rather die . . . and I mean that . . . than let him come near me."

She shivered as she spoke and put her hands up to her face, and her fears, imaginary or otherwise, were obviously very real to her.

Again some warning voice within Tyson told him to get out while there was still time.

It was difficult enough to help himself, let alone this girl with her lovely face, expensive clothes, and what was obviously a social background of some importance.

He stood looking at her and she took her hands from her face.

"Please . . ." she said, "I swear I will be no . . . trouble. I will go away as soon as I can . . . but I must have time to think . . . where I can . . . go."

It was perhaps because her eyes were misty with unshed tears that Tyson made up his mind.

He could not bear to see a woman cry, and while some critical part at the back of his mind told him he was mad, he found his lips saying:

"Very well. I will help you, but only, as you say, until you have had time to think."

Her whole face seemed to light up as if with an inner light and her eyes shone.

44

"Thank you! Thank you!"

"I have an uncomfortable feeling that I am going to get into a great deal of trouble over this," Tyson said.

"If you do in some way or another . . . I will make it up to you . . . all I want now is to get . . . away from . . . here."

Tyson smiled and picked up the only case which was left in the room.

"Then come along," he said, "but you had better bring the shawl you were talking about."

She did not seem surprised that he knew that was what she had said she must take with her.

She merely opened the wardrobe, took out her shawl and with it a bonnet which was decorated with ribbons that matched her gown.

"Have you anything else?" Tyson asked.

She looked around.

"No. That man took everything else and Sir Neville kept saying I must not forget my jewellery. I think he wanted that as much as he wanted me."

"I doubt it," Tyson replied dryly. "Now let us hurry away before anyone discovers what has happened to you."

"Yes . . . please let us . . . do that," the girl replied.

She edged rather nervously around Sir Neville's outstretched legs while Tyson walked over him.

They went out into the passage and he locked the door and put the key into his pocket.

"Let us hope they will not call you too early tomorrow morning," he said.

She gave a little gurgle of laughter as if she understood what he was meaning.

Then she sped ahead of him down the stairs to wait for him at the bottom a little nervously.

"What . . . what do we . . . do now?" she whispered.

"Wait here," he said.

He walked slowly and without haste into the courtyard.

Bill, as he expected, was sitting on the box, the reins in his hands looking towards the door from which he had emerged.

Tyson walked round the carriage until he was beside Bill, then he looked up at him.

"I have a message for you," he said in a low voice.

As Bill bent towards him to hear it Tyson dragged him off the box and onto the ground.

" 'Ere! Wot are ye doin'?" Bill demanded, only to be silenced in the same way as his employer and Jake had been.

Tyson dragged him across the yard and into the stable where the horses had been, throwing him down on the straw.

Then he went to the next stall to say:

"Come on, Salamanca."

The horse came towards him, he knotted the reins onto his neck and tucked the stirrups deftly one after the other into the girths.

Then he walked out into the courtyard with Salamanca following him.

He could see the girl watching him from the darkened doorway and he beckoned her.

She ran towards him and he opened the door of the carriage.

"What about your horse?" she asked in a whisper.

"He will follow," Tyson answered confidently, putting the case in beside her.

He shut her inside, climbed up onto the box and picked up the reins.

The pair of horses he was to drive must, he thought, have travelled quite a long way that day, for they were tired and stood quite docilely while their coachman was taken from them.

Tyson drove the carriage out of the yard and onto the road.

He looked back to see that Salamanca was

following, then he drove without haste through the village and back down the drive towards Revel Royal.

"I thought peace in England would be quiet and rather dull," he told himself as they went, "but I have certainly started my civilian career with an adventure which I anticipate may land me in prison, if I am not careful!"

He wondered what the penalty for abducting a minor was, and had the uncomfortable feeling that it was transportation!

Chapter 2

As Tyson drew up the horses at the main door, a man came running down the steps towards the carriage.

Tyson looked down at him in surprise, then exclaimed:

"Hawkins! I did not think you would get here so soon!"

The man drew himself up and saluted, and there was a broad smile on his face.

"It didn't take as long as I thinks, Sir," he remarked.

"I could not be more glad to see you!" Tyson said, putting down the reins and stepping down from the box of the carriage. "You might bring the luggage in first."

Hawkins went to the back of the carriage where the trunks had been strapped by Bill and Tyson opened the door.

There was just a moment's pause before the girl he had rescued stepped out and he thought perhaps she was shy.

Then she looked up at the house and exclaimed:

"How lovely! Does it belong to you?"

Revel Royal certainly looked very different in the pale light from a half-moon
than it had appeared earlier in the day.

The moonlight was glinting on what re-
mained of the diamond-casements and
there was a mystery in the shadows which
gave it a haunting beauty that Tyson remembered of old.

"It does not look so attractive inside," he
said, "but I do not intend to apologise for its
shortcomings."

"Of course not," the girl replied. "You
know how grateful I am to you for bringing
me here."

She walked up the steps and Tyson saw
there was a light in the Hall.

He turned back to Hawkins, who by now
had unstrapped the trunks from the back of
the carriage.

"What I want you to do, Hawkins,"
Tyson said, "is to take this carriage back to
the green. I expect you noticed it as you
came through the village?"

"I knows where 'tis, Sir."

"Just leave the horses there and come
away as quickly as possible. Do not let
anyone see you."

"Very good, Sir."

It was typical of the man who had served with him in the Peninsula and in France for the last six years, Tyson thought, that he asked no questions and carried out without comment, orders however unusual they might be.

"I will put Salamanca in the stable," Tyson said, "if there is one which is habitable."

"I'll do it, Sir," Hawkins replied. "It's all ready for him. I found some straw and he's slept in worse places — as we have."

Tyson found himself smiling at his servant.

There was a camaraderie which men found in war that he thought might be hard to translate into terms of peace, but for the moment the relationship between himself and Hawkins was a close understanding and a kind of satisfaction in being able to do things together.

"I will help you inside with the luggage," Tyson said.

He picked up one handle of the heavy leather trunk and Hawkins took the other, and they carried it up the steps and set it down in the Hall.

The girl was standing waiting for them and the candlelight made her fair hair seem to flicker with little flames of fire.

Once again Tyson found himself thinking it was not surprising that men wanted to marry her whether she was willing or not.

Hawkins brought in the rest of the luggage and said:

"I'll be off now, Sir. You'll find everything ready for you in what the old lady told me was called the 'Master Bedroom.' "

"Thank you, Hawkins," Tyson said, "but this lady will sleep there tonight."

"No, no!" the girl interposed. "I must not turn you out of your room."

"Hawkins and I are used to making the best of what is available," Tyson said. "I will see if my mother's room is habitable and tomorrow you shall move in there."

She looked at him with her large eyes which he thought in the candlelight were the blue of a stormy sea.

He had the feeling that she was willing to obey him because she wanted to express her gratitude by doing so.

At any rate, she made no further protests and he picked up the smaller piece of her luggage asking:

"Will this be enough for tonight?"

"Yes," she replied. "It is all I needed at the Inn. But my uncle thought the other trunks would be safer in my room than if they were left on the carriage all night."

"I am sure your uncle was right."

Tyson started to walk up the stairs and she followed him. Then he checked himself and went back to fetch one of the candles.

"I only arrived here today," he said, "and I am sure the passages are dark, even if the candles are lit in my room."

He noticed as he spoke, that she was looking around, and he was certain she had not missed the dust on everything, the windows in the Hall stuffed with rags where glass had been broken and the newels missing from the carved oak staircase.

"I have been away for thirteen years," he said, as if she had asked the question.

"I was sure you were a soldier even before I saw your servant was wearing a uniform."

"To which he is no longer entitled," Tyson said harshly.

Already the problem of what he was to do about Hawkins was in his mind.

Tomorrow he would have to tell the man again he could not afford him.

He had done so already before they left Dover, but Hawkins had insisted that he would come with him to Revel Royal and, to make sure Tyson expected him, he had kept back everything he possessed with the exception of enough things for the night.

"I've no plans, Sir," Hawkins had said.

"Me parents are dead and I'm homeless, so to speak. I'll see you into your house, and if then you've no use for me, I'll push on."

"It is not a question of having no use for you, Hawkins," Tyson replied, "it is just that I have no money with which to pay you, and as far as I can ascertain I shall be hard put to it to find enough food for Salamanca."

Even as he spoke, there had been an optimistic hope in his heart that things would not be as bad as he anticipated. But they had, in fact, turned out to be far worse.

He thought now, as he reached the top of the stairs and turned along the passage which led to what was known as the 'Master Suite', that he had been crazy to involve himself with a stranger like the girl who was following him.

The little money he had saved in France would last, if he was careful with it, only a few months. Then where would he turn for more?

He opened the door of what had been his father's room and saw as he had expected that Hawkins, or old Briggs, had left two candles burning on the chest-of-drawers above which there was a mahogany-framed mirror.

He therefore put the candle he carried

down on the table just outside the door and as he did so the girl passed into the bedroom to exclaim:

"What a wonderful bed! I have never seen anything like it!"

Tyson smiled, for he remembered it was the usual reaction of strangers when they first saw the huge four-poster in which it was believed King Charles II himself slept.

It was certainly very impressive with its carved and gilt posts and a canopy which rioted with angels and love-knots in the Restoration fashion.

Tonight with only two candles to light the room it was easy to miss the broken pieces of carving, the dust on the angels and the places where the gold had chipped away.

Also at a quick glance one did not notice that the embroidered curtains which hung at the back and skies were torn and that the valance around the bed had undoubtedly been chewed away by mice.

Tyson saw that Mrs Briggs had put clean sheets on the bed and there were pillows edged with lace which he remembered his mother had always used.

He put down the case he carried and undid the straps on each side of it.

"I hope you will be all right here," he said. "If you take my advice you will get into bed and try to forget everything that has happened until the morning."

"I will . . . try," the girl said a little doubtfully.

Her eyes were on his and once again he saw a beseeching expression in them.

"What is it?" he asked before she could speak.

"I do not . . . wish to be a . . . nuisance," she said, "but you will not be . . . far away . . . just in case something . . . frightens me?"

"If the next room is habitable, which I hope it is," Tyson answered, "I shall sleep there. Lock your door. That will give you a sense of security."

As he spoke he looked questioningly at the door, wondering if the lock was in the same state as the one on the front door.

It appeared to be in good condition and there was a key in it.

"I suppose," he said, after a moment's hesitation, "that I should ask you whether you would like anything to eat, but quite frankly I am doubtful if my hospitality can extend as far as that, at this hour of the night."

"No, I want nothing," the girl answered, "and thank you . . . thank you again for being so kind. I never thought anyone could be so . . . unexpectedly wonderful to a . . . stranger."

Tyson did not miss the little tremor in her voice as if she was not far from tears.

"Go to bed," he said. "Everything will seem better in the morning. Then we will hold a Council of War and decide what is best for you to do."

He reached out his hand to the door and asked:

"By the way — what is your name?"

There was a perceptible pause before the girl replied:

"My father . . . always called me . . . Vania."

"An unusual name," Tyson said, "and I am called Tyson."

He realised she did not wish to inform him of her surname and he thought that for the first time since he had met her she was being sensible and reserved.

He opened the door and passed through it.

"Goodnight, Vania!"

"Goodnight . . . Tyson."

He picked up the candle that he had left in the passage and carrying it walked into the next-door room.

It had been his mother's and as he entered it, he felt almost as if he was a little boy running to the person he loved best in the world and who he knew loved him.

But instead of the sweet fragrance he always associated with his mother's room and the scent of flowers, there was only the smell of dust and there was also something repressive in the fact that the furniture was covered with dust-sheets.

The curtains which hung at the sides of the bed had been lifted from the floor onto the mattress.

By the light of the candle Tyson walked across the floor of the room to open the wooden shutters, then the casements.

His mother's bedroom looked over the garden at the back of the house to where in the distance beyond the lawn and the flower-beds he could see in the moonlight the white gleam of a Grecian Temple.

It had been brought back from Greece by one of the Osbornes a hundred years ago and he remembered sitting in it with his mother while she told him stories of mythology which she had taught him to love as she did.

He had wanted to be like Apollo. He had wanted to have all the virtues of the gods who brought light and new thought to the men who worshipped them.

How long ago that all seemed now, he thought, and he had forgotten many of his aspirations when all he had been concerned with was killing the enemy.

He had thought of the French not as human beings but as objects of hatred because they were commanded by an ambitious maniac called Bonaparte.

Tyson turned from the window and felt that the warm, fresh night air swept away the smell of dust in his mother's room.

He walked to the bed, pushed the curtains off the mattress and pulled back the holland cover.

The bed was not made up and there were no sheets but several thick white blankets were neatly folded beside two swan's-down pillows.

He smiled and remembered he had slept in very much worse places and began to undress.

He told himself that when Hawkins returned from leaving the carriage and the horses on the green he would blow out the lights in the hall and doubtless push the bolt on the front door as old Briggs had asked him to do.

They were not likely to have burglars after all these years, but if they came there seemed to be very little of any value to take away.

But he could not be sure of that, and he told himself that tomorrow he would go over the house diligently with the idea of finding something he could sell.

He had the feeling there would be a great number of soldiers like himself who would wish to dispose of their possessions so that they could live and doubtless antique furniture and family portraits would be a glut on the market.

As he lay down on the mattress Tyson realised that he was very tired.

It had been a long day and he had not slept the night before when they had been busy embarking at Calais where his chief concern had been for Salamanca.

He had the feeling that he really ought to be thinking about the future. But as his eyes closed he knew that what he wanted more than anything else was to sleep and forget his problems.

His last thought before he finally drifted away into unconsciousness was that whatever the state of the house, whatever the difficulties he might find on the estate, it was all his.

Penniless or not, he was his own master!

In the next room Vania undressed slowly and pulling a very expensive lawn nightgown, inset with lace, from her leather box put it on and got into bed.

She left one candle burning beside her for the simple reason that she still felt a little frightened.

She had been fast asleep at the Inn when Sir Neville Buckley had burst into the room and ordered her to get dressed immediately.

"How dare you come here!" she had exclaimed, finding it hard to credit that any man, least of all Sir Neville, would dare to come into her room when she was in bed.

"Get up!" he said briefly, "and hurry! I am taking you away with me and we will be married tomorrow morning!"

Vania sat up in bed.

"I have no intention of marrying you. Kindly leave my bedroom."

He smiled and put down on a chest-of-drawers the lighted candle he had held in his hand.

"I intend to marry you," he said, "and all these protestations are not going to stop me. If you do not get dressed immediately, I will either help you, and I can assure you I am a most experienced lady's-maid, or I will take you with me as you are."

There was something in the way he spoke which told Vania all too clearly that he meant what he said, and while she sat looking at him her eyes very wide and frightened, he took a step towards her.

"No . . . no!" she cried. "I will . . . do what you . . . want."

"Then be quick about it!" he snapped.

"I . . . cannot . . . cannot get out of bed . . . when you are . . . looking at me."

"That is something you will not be able to prevent once we are married."

"W–we are not . . . married yet."

Vania meant her voice to sound defiant, but instead it sounded weak, frightened and very near to tears.

"I will shut my eyes," Sir Neville conceded.

She did not trust him, but there was nothing she could do but slip from the bed onto the floor and try to dress behind the high-backed chair on which she had left her clothes when she had retired.

"H–how can you . . . behave like this?" she asked when she had put on enough garments not to feel so embarrassingly naked.

"I told you I intended to be your husband," Sir Neville answered, "and I have not forgotten how insulting your uncle was to me."

"He . . . he did not . . . consider you to be a . . . suitable suitor."

"I am a very determined one!" Sir Neville retorted.

"P–please . . . do not take me . . . away,"

Vania pleaded. "Speak to my . . . uncle in the m—morning and perhaps you can persuade him to . . . change his mind."

Sir Neville laughed and it had not been a pleasant sound.

"You know perfectly well that your uncle will not listen to me, and I shall be turned away ignominiously as I was before."

He laughed again.

"No, no, Miss Clever! You are not going to catch me that way! I am taking you with me now. We will be married and all the talking can come later after you have become my wife."

"It will not be . . . legal as I am . . . under age," Vania protested.

"That will be for your uncle and his Solicitor to prove, but you will find they will accept the inevitable, once you are mine."

Vania knew only too well what he meant by that.

She felt herself shiver and knew despairingly that once she was in Sir Neville's clutches he would never let her go.

She had disliked him from the first moment they had met. He had paid her fulsome compliments, and she had known when she danced with him that he was unpleasant and had done her best for the rest of the evening to avoid him.

After that she seemed to meet him everywhere she went and it was only a question of time before he approached her uncle asking for her hand in marriage.

She had, in fact, been grateful when her uncle had said that Sir Neville was a fortune-hunter, an opportunist and a bounder, and he had given the servants instructions never to let him enter the house again.

She had thought that she was rid of Sir Neville, but there was a far worse menace in the shape of a suitor of whom her uncle did approve and to whom he had given his consent for their marriage.

It had been impossible for Vania to make her uncle understand that she had no wish to marry this particular man, or, for the moment, any other.

"You will marry whom I choose for you," her uncle said firmly, "and your aunt agrees with me that the sooner you settle down to married life, the better!"

Vania knew despairingly it was because her aunt was jealous of her, and her uncle found it a nuisance having to cope with her financial affairs.

Every night for the last two years since she had been forced to live with her uncle and aunt, she had cried out despairingly in the darkness for her father whom she had loved.

They had been so happy together and she regretted, she thought, every second of every day that she had not gone with him on his last voyage from which he had never returned.

Daringly, because Britain was at war even though the British Navy had command of the seas, Vania's father had wanted to visit the West Indies where he owned a great deal of property and had many financial interests.

It was not due to enemy action that the ship on which he was travelling back to England had been sunk, but because an unexpectedly severe storm had caused the mast to break and the ship had 'turned turtle'.

"If only I could have died with Papa," Vania said to herself over and over again, not only when she learnt of her father's death, but after she had gone to live with her uncle.

When she had learnt whom she was to marry, she had known that she must die rather than be touched by a man who revolted her to the point where he seemed as poisonous and as dangerous as a snake.

She had found herself wondering despairingly how she could either kill herself or escape from her uncle before they reached London.

Then when she found the only alternative was to be abducted by Sir Neville, she had thought that she was truly lost and there was no chance of her ever being saved from the fate which really was to her 'worse than death'.

Then incredibly, unexpectedly, a man she had never seen before had saved her!

Even now she could hardly realise that he had vanquished Sir Neville in his moment of triumph and taken her away while her uncle and aunt were still doped, so that she had escaped having to go to London and marry a man she loathed with every fibre of her being.

"Free! Free!" Vania whispered to herself.

She thought of the man who was sleeping next door to her and wondered how she could ever tell him how grateful she was.

He had seemed like an angel of deliverance or Perseus rescuing Andromeda from the sea-monster when he had knocked Sir Neville to the ground.

However, she knew how reluctant he was to do any more for her.

He had come to her rescue, but she felt that if he had had his own way he would have walked out of her room and she would never have seen him again — never even have known his name.

"Tyson!" she repeated to herself and thought it suited him.

He was handsome but in a different way from any other man she had seen.

There was something very strong, determined and clear-cut about his face and she thought it was perhaps because he had been a soldier and faced death for so many years.

He looked tense and as if every part of his body was alert.

He must be very strong, she thought, to have knocked out Sir Neville who was a tall and large man and to have done the same to the coachman who had been sitting on the box waiting to carry her and her luggage away.

It had all been quite a clever plot on the part of Sir Neville, she thought, for she knew that once she belonged to him it would have been very difficult for her uncle to declare the marriage invalid.

It would have caused a scandal and that was one thing her uncle would always avoid at any cost.

But Tyson had saved her.

She could see him now looking at her across the bedroom at the Inn with a reassuring smile on his lips and Sir Neville sprawling senseless at his feet.

It was hard to believe it had actually happened — one moment she had been menaced and insulted by Sir Neville forcing her to dress herself, and the next moment Perseus had appeared and the Monster was vanquished!

"Andromeda must have been very . . . very . . . grateful!" Vania said to herself, and fell asleep.

Vania awoke to find someone was pulling back the curtains and saw it was a very elderly woman with white hair.

She walked from the window to the bed to say:

"I've brought you a cup of tea, Miss, and there's a can of hot water in which you can wash."

Vania sat up in bed.

"Thank you," she said. "What time is it?"

"Nine o'clock, Miss. Master Tyson wouldn't have you called before as he thought you must be very tired."

"I was!" Vania admitted.

Now she felt clear-headed and bright after such a long sleep.

She poured out the tea that the old woman had set down beside her, noting that the silver pot needed cleaning, but the china was very fine, although there was a chip out of the saucer.

The old woman moving very slowly un-locked the door into the passage, brought in a brass can which had obviously been left outside and carried it to the wash-hand stand.

Vania realised she had entered the room through another door which doubtless com-municated with the room next door.

Vania remembered that last night she had taken her host's room and he had been forced to find another place to sleep.

"Your master is very kind," she said aloud.

"It's glad we be to have him back," Mrs Briggs replied. "There'll be many who have not returned from that wicked war."

"There will indeed!" Vania agreed, "but now we have peace and everyone can be happy again."

"That's what we all hopes," Mrs Briggs said. "Is there anything more I can do for you, Miss?"

"No, thank you."

"There'll be some breakfast downstairs in the Dining-Room, Miss, when you're aready for it," Mrs Briggs said.

"Thank you," Vania said again, and watched the old woman move from the room.

'She is very old,' she thought, and in contrast felt very young.

Then because she was excited, because she suddenly realised that she was in the midst of what was a breathtaking adventure, she jumped out of bed.

'Papa would enjoy this,' she thought as she poured the hot water into the basin.

Her father had always been adventurous, always interested in something new, always looking for new horizons.

He had in consequence wanted her to live a more conventional life.

"Next year when you are seventeen," he had said to her, "I will take you to London and you shall make your début."

He looked at her with a smile as he added:

"I do not mind taking a bet that you will be acknowledged as the most beautiful debutante of the Season, and undoubtedly, although it will infuriate me, the Bucks of St James's will toast you as an 'Incomparable'."

"I hope so, Papa!" Vania cried.

"You will give me some anxious moments," her father said. "At the same time, I shall be very proud."

Vania had given a little cry.

"I want you to be proud of me, Papa! I want everyone to say how clever you are to have a beautiful daughter besides all the other things you have achieved."

Her father had laughed.

"You will always be my greatest achievement, my dearest," he said, "and there are many things you and I can do together before you get married."

"I shall only marry if I find a man as clever, as handsome and as lovable as you, Papa!"

Her father had laughed again.

"That, I am sure, will be impossible!" he said, "but perhaps there will be a 'runner-up' whom I can tolerate."

"I shall never marry anyone," Vania went on, "unless he is as wonderful as you and I really love him."

Her father had kissed her.

"I promise you one thing, my darling, you shall never marry anyone you do not love. That to my mind would be a hell on earth."

That was what Vania had thought it would be too, but what was the point of telling her uncle so?

"Love is for peasants," he had said firmly. "Aristocrats and those who are sensible arrange a marriage which is advantageous to both parties."

"But supposing I hate the man you have chosen for me?" Vania argued.

"Women learn to obey their husbands,"

her uncle said harshly, "and romantic love only exists in the minds of poets and idiots."

This conversation had taken place before her uncle finally produced the man she was to marry and she might have anticipated that she would hate him.

"Now no-one knows where I am and Uncle Lionel will not think of looking for me here," she told herself. "Why should he? And if he hears that Sir Neville was at the Inn, perhaps he will assume that he has, in fact, spirited me away."

It was certainly an intriguing possibility and as soon as she was dressed Vania hurried down the stairs not only intent on finding her breakfast, because she was hungry, but also because she wanted to see Tyson.

Now in the bright sunlight that was pouring through the broken windows and the open front door she could see what a lamentable condition the house was in, even though she thought everything about it was quaint and attractive.

Hawkins was in the Hall.

"Good-morning, Miss!" he said. "If you'll go into the Dining-Room I'll bring your breakfast for you."

"Where is . . . Mr Tyson?" Vania asked, hesitating over how to refer to her host, knowing that as she had only given him her Christian name, he had deliberately done the same.

"The Master's out in the stables, Miss," Hawkins replied. "I'll be joining him after I've fetched your breakfast and I'll tell him you're downstairs."

"I will come and join you when I know where the stables are," Vania answered.

Because she was in a hurry she ate the boiled egg as quickly as she could and drank the cup of coffee so quickly that it threatened to burn her throat.

Then she ran along the passage and out through the front door and following Hawkins' directions found herself in the stables.

She saw at once that they were in an even worse condition than the house. The yard was thick with weeds and a great number of red tiles which had covered the sloping roofs of the stables were on the ground.

Tyson was quite unconcernedly brushing down Salamanca and whistling as he did so.

He must have heard Vania's footsteps, light though they were, and before she could speak he turned his head to say:

"Good-morning, Vania!"

She was standing in the open doorway of the stable and the sunshine seemed to halo her hair. She looked, Tyson thought, like a visitor from another Planet.

Never had he thought anyone could be so small, so exquisite, look exactly like a piece of Dresden china, and yet be a real person.

"I have slept disgracefully late!" Vania said. "May I help you?"

Tyson laughed.

"I hardly think your gown is very appropriate for this sort of work."

He thought as he spoke that it was certainly a very pretty gown and extremely becoming.

Gowns were very much more elaborate than they had been at the beginning of the century. They were still high-waisted, but no longer transparent, the modern young woman would dampen her muslin to make it cling almost indecently to her figure.

Now the skirts outlined the hips and swirled out at the hem. They were embroidered or bedecked with lace and Vania had some very pretty puff-sleeves on her gown edged with muslin frills.

"I do not mind getting dirty," she said carelessly.

"I should hate you to do so," Tyson replied, "and besides have you thought that your clothes, even though you seem to have an abnormal amount of them, may have to last you for a long time?"

"I had not thought of that," Vania answered.

As she spoke she came further into the stall and passing Tyson walked to Salamanca's head to pat his neck.

"I suppose you know," she said to him in a soft little voice, "that you are the most beautiful horse I have ever seen, and Salamanca is exactly the right name for you."

"I christened him after the battle," Tyson said, "in which he distinguished himself."

"As you did?"

"Of course!"

"You were decorated?"

There was a pause, then Tyson answered:

"As a matter of fact I was!"

"I knew it! I knew it!" Vania said. "You are a hero, and only a hero could have saved me as you did last night."

Tyson straightened himself.

"I think, Vania," he said, "the sooner we have a little talk about you and your future, the better!"

Her eyes twinkled at him and he saw there was a dimple on the side of her mouth.

"Now you are getting authoritative and prosy," she said. "You are exactly like my School-Mistress who always said she

75

wanted 'a little talk' when she was in fact going to find fault."

"I promise you not to do that," Tyson replied, "but quite frankly, I am worried about you."

"It is such a lovely day I do not want to be worried," Vania said. "I am safe, I am free, and I am happy! What more can I ask of life?"

Tyson smiled.

"A great deal more. And that is why we have to talk, you and I, and decide what is best for you."

Vania turned her face away from him and put her cheek against Salamanca's head.

She decided in that moment that she would be very clever and tell him nothing.

If he knew who she was, if he knew where she was supposed to be going when she reached London, he might be difficult. He might insist on getting in touch with either her uncle or the man it had been intended she should marry.

'He has no idea who I am,' she thought, 'but I know who he is!'

She had seen at the bottom of the picture in her bedroom an inscription which read: "*Sir Thomas Osborne*", and she thought she detected in the face of the man who looked at her, a likeness to Tyson.

"He is Tyson Osborne," Vania told herself. "If I am clever I can encourage him to try to keep his identity secret and then it will be easy for me to keep mine."

Tyson was emptying away the pail of dirty water with which he had been washing Salamanca.

Now he put the brush he had been using on the window-ledge.

He had taken off his coat and he put it on again as if it gave him a mantle of authority.

"Come along, Vania," he said. "Let us get the unpleasantness over, then perhaps later you would like to ride with me over my estate. I want to see it for myself."

"Are you suggesting we ride Salamanca together?" Vania enquired. "I am quite certain he would find it no hardship to carry us both."

"I have another horse," Tyson replied.

"Where?"

He glanced at her and she followed him to a stall which was some distance away from Salamanca's.

She realised why the horses were not nearer to each other when she could see daylight through the roof above the two stalls next to Salamanca's.

"Hawkins bought this horse for a mere song," Tyson explained, "because the man whose charger he was, was a spoilt young swine who has a large stable waiting for him in this country. He decided he could not be bothered with the difficulties involved in conveying him there."

There was so much contempt in Tyson's voice that Vania knew he loved horses as she did, and she moved into the stall where a fine-looking grey was being brushed down by Hawkins.

"He is beautiful!" she said, "but not as magnificent as Salamanca."

"That is exactly what I thought," Tyson agreed, "but it was a good buy, Hawkins."

"I thought you'd think so, Sir, and only one gentleman was bidding against me. But he'd had too much to drink and so he forgets what he was after!"

Tyson laughed.

"Do you know what this horse is called?"

"Of course I do, Sir, and perhaps I should add it was me own choice."

"What you are saying," Vania intervened, "is that you have renamed him."

"Quite right, Miss," Hawkins agreed, "and Vittoria's his name."

"Another battle!" Vania exclaimed.

"And a very unpleasant one," Tyson said dryly.

"But we survived, Sir. That's why I've

always remembered it," Hawkins said. "Survived! But there were moments, I don't mind telling you, when I thought we was for it!"

Tyson smiled.

He was remembering that the French Army had been 58,000 strong and that King Josef had made every effort to escape with his baggage-train into the guerilla-haunted mountains.

There had been the usual anxiety over four Divisions which were delayed and the timing of the attack was made more difficult by the fact that the 7th Division appeared to be lost so that the assault on the bridges hung fire.

Looking back Tyson could remember so vividly those awful moments of tension and indecision.

Then at last everything began to move and almost before they could realise it with the guns shaking in the earth and the muskets flashing like lightning the Battle of Vittoria was over and he and Hawkins were both alive without even a scratch, even though a great number of their comrades were dead.

Yes, he told himself, like Hawkins, he would remember the Battle of Vittoria while a great many of the others would slip from his mind.

"It is a lovely name for a lovely horse," he heard Vania say and thought she seemed to know how much her approval would please Hawkins.

"Come on, Vania," he said aloud, "you shall ride Vittoria this afternoon, but now I intend to talk to you although I am quite aware that you are trying to avoid it."

"Not really," Vania said, "it is just that there are so many other things to do and talking is such a bore!"

"Boring or not, this is important," Tyson said firmly.

He walked over the weeds towards the house and reaching the entrance to the stables looked back to see if Vania was following him.

She was, holding up her gown so that the grasses would not damage it.

"Can you manage?" he asked.

"Of course!" she replied, "but you worried me by saying my gowns will have to last me for a very long time, so I am being careful!"

"That sounds sensible, at any rate."

"This is a lovely, lovely house, and I think you are very lucky to own it," Vania said.

"I am worrying what I can do about my house, just as I am worrying what I can do about you."

"I am not in such a grievous state," she said mischievously.

"I am not certain about that!" he replied.

They were walking from the stables along the front of the house towards the steps.

"I want to go down to the lake," Vania said suddenly. "It is so beautiful. There ought to be white swans looking majestic and skimming over the water!"

"There used to be," Tyson said. "I expect they died or flew away as there was no-one to feed them."

The note of pain in his voice was inescapable.

"You love it, do you not?" Vania asked.

He did not answer for a moment, then he said:

"Yes, I love it! But what can I do to keep it?"

"May I say something . . . seriously?" she enquired.

He looked at her almost as if he had been thinking of something else and not realised she was still beside him.

"Of course."

"You may think I am pretending to be a prophetess but I am convinced that if you set your mind to it, you can do . . . anything you . . . want to do."

"How can you be sure of that?" Tyson
asked.

"Because you are the sort of man who
would always be victorious. Last night you
reminded me of my father, and now I know
you are very like him. Papa always got what
he . . . wanted in life and you will do the . . .
same."

"I wish I could believe you," Tyson said,
"but, Vania, we both have to take our heads
out of the clouds and face facts, hard and
unpalatable though they may be."

"Now we are back to the School-Room!"
Vania exclaimed in disgust.

Because he could not help it, Tyson
laughed.

Chapter 3

Tyson walked towards the Library thinking that it was a most suitable place in which to speak seriously to Vania.

He might have guessed that she would read his thoughts, for when he turned round he found she was standing just inside the door.

"Do I sit or stand, Sir?" she asked in a demure manner.

Tyson smiled, at the same time he answered firmly:

"Do not be obstructive, Vania. You know this is for your own good."

"Which means inevitably that it will be extremely unpleasant."

He did not reply and she walked towards him to sit down on the sofa, still assuming the attitude of a young girl in front of a School-Master, her back very straight, her hands in her lap.

"When I brought you here last night,"

Tyson began, "you persuaded me that I was saving you from an unpleasant marriage."

"That is true."

"I believe you," Tyson said, "but you know as well as I do that you cannot stay here alone with me. As soon as possible you must go to some relation or a friend whom you can trust."

"I told you last night that I know I can trust you," Vania said sweetly.

"If your parents were alive," Tyson replied, "they would be horrified, and quite rightly so, that you are staying unchaperoned with a man you met only by chance."

"I know Papa would have liked you," Vania said defensively, "and if he was alive he would never force me into marrying anybody I did not love. He always said so."

"Let me speak to your uncle," Tyson suggested. "I will tell him the position in which you found yourself and I am quite certain I can make him see reason."

"That is something you could never do!" Vania said positively. "My uncle is a self-opinionated, stupid bore who thinks no-one is ever right except himself."

"He is still your Guardian," Tyson replied, "and as such entitled to your consideration. You cannot just disappear and leave him wondering where you are."

"I think he will be delighted to be rid of me."

"What I suggest," Tyson went on as if she had not spoken, "is that I talk to your uncle and, before I tell him where you are, persuade him to promise me that he will not make you marry anyone you do not wish to."

"You really believe he would keep his promise?" Vania asked. "Of course he would not! I know my uncle!"

"Nevertheless I must see him," Tyson said, "so please tell me his name and where I am likely to find him."

Vania rose from the sofa on which she was sitting and walked across the room to the window.

She stood for a moment looking out at the lake before she remarked:

"I am happy here and I have decided to help you in putting your house in order."

Tyson's eyes were watching the sunshine on her hair, then he answered:

"I have already explained that, much as I should like you to be my guest indefinitely, it is impossible both from your point of view and from mine."

"I have heard why you think I should not stay with you," Vania replied, "but perhaps

85

Mrs Briggs, or Hawkins, would constitute a chaperon if you are really worried about your reputation."

"I am not worrying about my reputation, as well you know," Tyson said sharply, "but yours."

"That does not concern me in the slightest," Vania answered, "so there is no need for it to concern you."

"Now look here . . ." Tyson began.

He stopped.

"You are being deliberately obstructive," he said accusingly. "Give me the name of your uncle and leave the rest to me."

"That is something which I have no intention of doing," Vania said quietly. "My name is Vania, and when you rescued me you did not stop to ask for my credentials. You merely behaved like a hero or, as I have thought since in my mind, like Perseus."

Tyson smiled as if he could not help it.

"If I remember the story aright," he said, "he was then forced to marry Andromeda and I hardly think that I would be a satisfactory husband at the moment."

"Why not?" Vania asked. "I would certainly rather marry you than Sir Neville and be very much more willing to do so than . . ."

She pressed her lips together quickly as if

86

she had almost uttered the name of the man who her uncle had intended to be her husband.

Tyson moved to the desk in the centre of the Library and sat down.

He opened a drawer, found a piece of paper and dipped a quill-pen into the ink-well.

"Now let us stop play-acting. Tell me your uncle's name."

He spoke severely in the tone he had used so often to good effect when confronted with a soldier who needed reprimanding.

But Vania, sitting on the edge of the window-sill, merely laughed.

"Now you are back to being a School-Master," she said. "No . . . how stupid of me! Of course, you are the Commander-in-Chief, the man who has soldiers ready to click their heels and salute before they obey your slightest whim. How annoying for you that I am a woman and not a man!"

Her tone was mocking and her lips were smiling.

Tyson looked at her.

"I do not know what your education was like," he said, "but one thing was obviously omitted and that was a good spanking!"

"Is that what you are suggesting I might receive from you?" Vania asked provocatively.

87

"It is a distinct possibility," Tyson said grimly.

Vania clasped her hands together.

"Oh, dear! Oh, dear!" she cried. "Who will rescue me now? Last night you came in the nick of time! I am just wondering whether I ought to appeal to the chivalrous feelings of old Briggs, or whether I should tempt Hawkins away from his obvious loyalty to you."

"You are an irritating brat!" Tyson thundered, "and I cannot think why I was such a fool as to encumber myself with you."

He was feeling frustrated by Vania's attitude and he glared at her. Then as she smiled at him from across the room he found his irritation evaporating.

He sat back in the chair which his father had always used and said in a very different tone:

"If you will not think of yourself then I shall have to ask you to think of me. If you want the truth, Vania, I cannot afford to keep you."

She raised her eyebrows but she did not speak and he went on:

"I have come back to England with very little money to find, as you see, the house is crumbling about my ears, the Briggses have used up all their savings and have only stayed on because they had nowhere else to go. I have already dismissed Hawkins because I cannot afford to pay him."

He paused and Vania listening knew how much he disliked having to say this.

Then he continued:

"I am going round the house today to see if there is anything I can sell, but I know already there is nothing that will fetch more than a guinea or two."

"Then what will you do?" Vania asked.

"I do not know," Tyson answered, "but I hope I have made it clear to you that I cannot afford any more mouths to feed."

He thought as he spoke that he was being somewhat crude, but he was really thinking that only the hard truth would make Vania face the fact that she must return to her uncle or to some relative who would take care of her.

There was a little silence after he had spoken. Then Vania said:

"I can pay for my . . . keep. I have not much money with me, but my jewels are considered to be valuable."

Tyson rose from the chair in which he had been sitting.

"I have not reached the stage," he said in any icy voice, "where I am forced to accept money from a woman."

"Now you are just being proud and pompous," Vania flashed at him. "I am not suggesting I should give you money, but merely pay for my board and lodging."

"The answer is categorically no!"

"Supposing I refuse to leave?" Vania enquired. "Will you turn me out into the snow and lock the front door on me?"

Before he could answer she laughed.

"One thing about this house," she said, "is that one could always sneak in through a broken window or the doors which have no locks."

"Will you talk sense?" Tyson ejaculated. "You cannot stay here! I have made that clear, and I cannot believe that you wish to be an embarrassment and an encumbrance to me."

"Am I . . . really that?" Vania asked a little wistfully.

"You will be — if you do not leave soon."

"How soon?"

"Vania, be sensible!" Tyson pleaded. "Give me your uncle's name or the name of one of your relatives who might be prepared to house you."

She turned away from him once again to look out of the window.

It suddenly struck him how small and childish she was, and he found himself thinking that it would be very difficult for her to hold out against her uncle's determination to get her off his hands by marriage.

It would also be impossible for her to manage alone.

He walked across the room to stand beside her.

"I am trying to help you, Vania," he said gently. "I want to help you. Please let me."

For a moment there was no response, then she turned her face to look up at him.

"That is unfair," she said in a low voice. "I can fight you when you are ordering me about, but when you coax me it is . . . far more . . . difficult."

There was something so young in her words and so unexpectedly pathetic in her expression that Tyson capitulated.

"I do not want to be unreasonable," he said. "Shall we postpone the rest of this conversation for twenty-four hours? That should give you time to think of a solution."

He saw the light come into her eyes as she said:

"Can we do . . . that?"

"I am agreeable — if you are."

"I am not so much concerned about my future," she said impulsively, "as with my present! Because you saved me, I am free of my past."

"That is a very irresponsible way of looking at life," Tyson said, "but I have given you a promise that we will let twenty-four hours pass before we speak about it again."

"Thank you . . . thank you!" Vania cried, "and now until luncheon time let us go and explore your house. It is so fascinating, I want to see every corner of it."

She slipped her hand into his as she spoke and started to pull him across the Library to the door.

Although Tyson had the feeling that he should resist her blandishments, he capitulated again.

Riding back to Revel Royal late in the afternoon they were both of them rather silent.

Vania had been in high spirits when after a light luncheon they had set off to explore the estate.

It consisted, Tyson told her, of a thousand acres, and his father had farmed five hundred of them. The rest was let to two farmers, one on the north side of the property and one to the west.

They rode north first because that, Tyson explained, was where the larger farm was situated.

He remembered as a boy the farmer not only kept cattle but grew fields of golden corn and feathery barley which his father had always said were the finest in the whole County.

Tyson was not surprised to find his own land had been left lying uncultivated and was overgrown with weeds and nettles.

He had learnt from Briggs that on his father's death the younger members of the estate workers had either joined the Army or had found jobs on neighbouring estates, while the older men had found great difficulty in obtaining other employment.

Tyson had lain awake all night puzzling as to what had happened after his father's death to the money he owned, which although not a great fortune, had always been more than enough for their needs.

The letters from his father's Solicitors, that reached him spasmodically while on active service, had been difficult to understand simply because they did not contain the information he needed.

"I will go and see Chessington to-morrow," he promised himself, but he thought first it would be wise to have a general idea of the state of his property.

There was no question of what had happened to the big farm on the north side.

Tyson was apprehensive as he and Vania rode over fields that had not been ploughed or planted and saw the farm and its buildings in the distance.

As they drew nearer it was easy to see the sorry state of the roofs, the boarded-up windows and a general air of dilapidation.

"It looks so sad," Vania said in a low voice.

Tyson knew it was not only sad, it was disastrous from his point of view, and it was a relief to find there was actually somebody living on the smaller farm.

The farmer was old now and so was his wife.

"Oi've done what Oi could, Master Tyson," he said, "but everythin's been agin' Oi. Me two sons were killed, one after th'other. Oi couldn't afford to hire men, so there be only meself to see t'everythin'."

"An' him not well," his wife chimed in. "He's never been strong, as ye must remember, Master Tyson."

Tyson did not, but he was too kind to say so.

"Oi've paid no rent," the farmer said, " 'cause there just wasn't th' money an' there were no-un as Oi could ago to for repairs."

Looking around the farm, Tyson knew that hundreds of pounds would need to be spent on the roofs and the barns while the house itself was barely habitable.

When he left the farmer gave him a whole list of requirements that were urgently needed.

Because both the farmer and his wife looked at him eagerly as if they relied on him to save them, Tyson had not the heart to take away their last hope by saying that he was in no better state than they were.

"What can you do for them?" Vania asked as they rode away.

"Nothing!" he replied savagely, "but I had not the courage to tell them so."

She rode on for a little while in silence before she said:

"I think you hoped that the rent from your two farms would help you to repair your own house."

"I thought it might help me to live there for a little while longer," Tyson replied, "but as you see, I was mistaken."

Now there was a bitter note in his voice that had not been there before and Vania glanced at him swiftly before she looked away again.

When Revel Royal came in sight Tyson drew in his horse. The house standing on high ground with its roof silhouetted against the sky, looked in the distance very lovely.

It was as it had stood for hundreds of years, and yet now, Tyson thought angrily, it would crumble slowly into the ground and there was nothing he could do to prevent it.

As if she understood what he was feeling Vania said nothing. Then when they rode on again, she started to talk gaily and inconsequentially of things which had nothing to do with the estate or them personally.

By the time they reached the house Tyson's eyes had lost their pain and she had made him laugh.

They put the horses in the stables and as there was no sign of Hawkins, Vania insisted on rubbing down Vittoria.

"I always used to look after my pony when I was a little girl," she said, "and perhaps when you no longer want me . . . I can get a job in a racing stable. You have to admit I am a good rider!"

"I have never said I do not want you," Tyson replied, "I said you could not stay with me for a number of excellent reasons which I will not repeat."

He finished attending to Salamanca and was standing in Vittoria's stall watching Vania attending to the horse.

She smiled at him over the grey's back.

"You are very precise and particular in

choosing your words," she said. "It rather becomes you."

"What do you mean by that?"

"Anyone can see you have been in the Army," she answered. "Your mind is so spick and span, so conscientious and above all so punctilious."

"I think what you are saying, although it sounds complimentary, is exactly the opposite," Tyson replied. "As I have told you before, you are an irritating brat and I am never quite certain when you are teasing me or being serious."

"I am serious when I say I like a lot of things about you," Vania replied, "and one day, if you are very good, I will tell you what they are."

"You infuriate me," Tyson replied, "and it is a very good thing for you that you are a girl and not a boy. But come along. I am hungry, and let us hope that Mrs Briggs has tea waiting for us."

There was tea and it reminded Tyson of the teas he had had when he was a boy. He thought as he saw Vania tucking into home-made bread crisp from the oven, that nothing could be more delicious.

"What are you going to do now?" she asked when they had both finished eating.

"I am going to finish my tour of the

house," Tyson answered, "because to-morrow I intend to ride into Canterbury to see my Solicitor."

"Why have you not seen him already?"

"Because I arrived only yesterday afternoon, a short time before I came to the *Dog and Duck* with, as you know, disastrous results from my point of view."

She made a little grimace at him and said:

"What made you visit the Inn?"

"I think really I wanted to 'drown my sorrows' after I had seen Revel Royal," Tyson said honestly, "and I certainly did not mean to embroil myself in the dramatic events following a mere desire for a glass of wine."

"Are you sorry that you did not . . . stay at . . . home?"

He knew she was asking the question because she really wished to know the answer, and her eyes looking into his told him that she was afraid that he was, in fact, regretting that he had rescued her.

"I will spoil you," Tyson replied, "by telling you I am very glad first that I went to the *Dog and Duck* and secondly that I did not leave ten minutes earlier."

Vania gave a little cry and clasped her hands together.

"Supposing you had?" she asked. "Supposing you had not overheard Sir Neville giving instructions to his confederates? What would have . . . happened to me by . . . now?"

There was a note of real fear in the question and Tyson said quickly:

"Forget it! I was there and let us hope that Sir Neville is now suffering from a severe headache and a sore jaw."

Vania gave a little laugh.

"You hit him so hard. I would not be surprised if you dislodged half his teeth!"

"I can only hope that I dislodged the lot!" Tyson replied. "It will teach him, if nothing else, to be careful who overhears his plans next time he tries to abduct a lovely lady."

"Supposing he . . . tries to find . . . me?" Vania asked in a low voice.

"I hardly think he will look for you in this village," Tyson replied. "He is much more likely to start looking further afield."

"Yes, of course," Vania said, "but I think it would be a mistake for me to go anywhere where I am likely to be seen by people . . . in case he makes . . . enquiries about me."

Tyson looked at her sharply.

He thought perhaps she was trying to make him say he must continue to hide her for longer than he had intended.

Then he knew by the expression on her face and in her eyes, which he thought were transparently clear and very young, that she was, in fact, very frightened of Sir Neville just as she was terrified of the man her uncle wished her to marry.

"What the devil am I to do about the girl?" he asked himself and for the moment there was no answer.

The interview Tyson had with Mr Chessington, the Senior Partner of Chessington, Latham and Odburn, left him even more depressed than he had been the previous day.

He had ridden into Canterbury and with only a few minutes delay was shown into the inner sanctum of the office which he re-membered visiting on several occasions with his father, although Mr Chessington usually came to Revel Royal.

He had always been a dried-up, withered little man with a deeply lined face and grey hair, and in the thirteen years that Tyson had been away, he seemed not to have changed at all in appearance.

"My dear Major Dale!" he exclaimed when Tyson was shown into the office. "I am delighted to see you — really delighted! In fact I was sure you would soon be re-turning to England, now that the war is over."

Tyson shook his hand and sat down in a chair on the other side of the desk.

"I have returned in not very agreeable circumstances," he said without any preliminaries.

"I was afraid, very afraid you would be shocked at what you found at Revel Royal," Mr Chessington said, shaking his head, "and I assure you, I did everything in my power to prove your father and mother's marriage."

"I am not only interested in proving my legitimacy," Tyson said, "but in discovering the whereabouts of my father's money."

"It is a great mystery," Mr Chessington replied, "for which there seems to be no explanation."

"Tell me what happened," Tyson asked. "I am, as you are aware, completely in the dark."

"I explained everything to you in my letter," Mr Chessington said.

"If you gave me any explanation, it was in a letter I did not receive, but that is not surprising. We were moving all the time and mail from England was often either delayed for months at a time or did not arrive at all."

"Dear me, I am sorry to hear that."

"Tell me what happened," Tyson asked quietly.

"As you know, your father was always

having what he called 'hunches'," Mr Chessington began, "especially where his financial affairs were concerned."

"That is true," Tyson agreed, remembering that it was his father's 'hunches' that had created his fortune in the first place.

"About three months before his death," Mr Chessington went on, "your father had a 'hunch' that the Southern County and Canterbury Bank would close its doors."

"Did he tell you so?" Tyson enquired.

Mr Chessington nodded.

"He came here on the very day he had been to the Bank and drawn out everything he possessed."

"Everything?" Tyson enquired.

"Every penny is what he said," Mr Chessington replied, "and he added, 'Chessington, if you have any money in that Bank, I would advise you to remove it. I know in my bones that it is on the verge of collapse!' "

"And was it?" Tyson asked.

"I could hardly believe my own eyes," Mr Chessington replied, "when a month later I read in the newspapers that the Bank could not meet its liabilities."

"So my father was right."

"Completely and absolutely right."

"Where did he take his money?"

"That is just the point — he did not tell me!"

There was silence for a moment, then Tyson asked:

"You are quite certain he did not say anything that would give you a hint as to what he intended to do?"

Again Mr Chessington shook his head.

"I assure you," he said in his precise voice, "I have gone over and over in my mind the conversation I had with your father not once but a thousand times, trying to recall if he gave me any indication of his intentions. I suppose at the time I was so stunned by what he told me that it never struck me to enquire."

"So the money has vanished," Tyson said in a hard voice, "just as any reference to my father and mother's marriage has vanished."

"I have made enquiries," Mr Chessington said, "at every Church in the vicinity."

"They may not have been married locally," Tyson remarked. "When they ran away they disappeared for several years before they came back to live at Revel Royal."

"I always understood from your father, but I may have been mistaken," Mr Chessington said, "that they went abroad."

"Yes, that is correct," Tyson said, "in which case they may have left England before they married."

"It has, of course, been impossible for us to make enquiries at Calais or anywhere else in France," Mr Chessington said, "but it would be possible now that the war is over."

Tyson was silent.

He was thinking that his father would have married his mother at the first opportunity.

He had loved her in a way that made Tyson know instinctively that he would have thought it sacrilege to make her his, without the blessing of the Church.

What was more, she was a Parson's daughter!

"Would the Churches in this district have married them without the permission of my mother's father?" he asked Mr Chessington.

"I think in those days," the Solicitor replied, "things were much more lax than they are at the moment. The Marriage Act had not been introduced and there were all sorts of Chapels like the one in Mayfair where Parsons would perform marriages without even bothering to keep a Register."

"Yes, of course," Tyson agreed. "I thought of that when you wrote to me in

France telling me that you could find no record of the marriage."

"Knowing your father, dear boy," Mr Chessington said in a voice that had an unexpectedly warm note in it, "I am absolutely convinced that he and your mother were properly married, but you know as well as I do that legally one has to have proof."

"I know that," Tyson said, "especially when there is someone like my uncle determined to grab the title and the estates to which he has no right."

Tyson spoke violently because he had always disliked his uncle.

He knew that George Dale had been greedily impatient to grasp at the opportunity of installing himself in the position to which he had not been born.

Any decent person would have waited until the war was over and Tyson had returned to England to prove his own rights.

But not his Uncle George!

As if he knew what he was thinking, Mr Chessington said quietly:

"Now you are home, Major, I hope you will go on searching not only to prove yourself your grandfather's rightful heir, but also to clear your mother's name."

"That is what I want to do, and I intend to do," Tyson said. "The only difficulty is how

I can live in the meantime."

"I can understand your problem," Mr Chessington agreed, "but I must tell you I have been in touch with every Bank in the County, for I was quite sure your father would have gone to one of the large, well-known ones, but they all denied any knowledge of him as a client. I also sent two of my most experienced clerks to Revel Royal to search the house from attic to cellar."

Tyson did not speak and Mr Chessington continued:

"What is so extraordinary is that there were no important papers to be found at all, not in your father's desk or anywhere else in the house."

"Do you think he might have hidden them?" Tyson asked.

"I imagine we shall find everything we want to know when we find the money," Mr Chessington replied.

"Have you any idea how much there should be?"

"A very considerable sum. Your father was not only a rich man, but also an extremely clever one. I knew of some of the investments he made over the years, and they were always wise and always justified his 'hunches'."

"Well, I suppose if he had not had one of his hunches and he had left his money in the Southern County and Canterbury Bank I should be in exactly the same position I am in now."

"That may be a philosophical way of looking at it," Mr Chessington said, "but it does not solve your problem."

"No, it does not," Tyson agreed. "All I can do is to search as you have done, and pray that I shall be more successful."

"I shall be praying the same thing," Mr Chessington said. "I have known you, since you were a little boy, and I have followed your career with great interest. When I heard you were decorated at the Battle of Salamanca I was as delighted as if you had been my own son."

"Thank you," Tyson said quietly. "I must also thank you for all you have done on my behalf. There is, I regret to say, no chance at the moment of my being able to pay your fees."

Mr Chessington looked embarrassed.

"I do not want to help you for what I can get out of it, Major. I was very fond of your father, and I would like to see Revel Royal restored to the state it was in when he lived there."

"That is what I would like to see too,"

Tyson said, "and more than anything else I want to prove that my mother was not the despicable creature whom my uncle has branded by declaring me illegitimate."

Tyson spoke with a violence behind his words that was all the more effective because he did not raise his voice.

"May I promise you," Mr Chessington said, "that I will help you in every way that is within my power."

Arriving home, Tyson not only felt warmed by his contact with the Solicitor, but he also had a determination within himself that gave him a power he had never felt before.

He would not be beaten. He would not allow his uncle to triumph by an action which he thought was so despicable that there were hardly words in which to describe it.

Anyone who had known his mother, anyone, too, who had known his father, would be aware that it was completely out of character for two such people, however much they might dislike the Social World, to live in what was known as 'sin' or to bring their only child into the world without a name.

It would have been against every instinct

in their bodies and every aspiration of their souls.

Tyson had learned his prayers at his mother's knee and all through his life he would remember her going to Church on Sundays and as soon as he was old enough, taking him with her.

He also could never recall a Church Festival, Christmas, Easter, or Whitsun when his father and mother did not attend Communion Service in the little grey stone Church in the village.

It was inconceivable to think they could have knelt at the altar as man and wife unless in the eyes of God it was right for them to do so.

"I will find the proof of their marriage," Tyson told himself, "if I have to spend my whole life searching for it."

He knew as he saw Revel Royal ahead of him that he would dedicate himself to a crusade of his own just as he dedicated himself during the war to vanquishing the tyrant who had embroiled all Europe in bloodshed.

He rode Salamanca round to the stables, unsaddled him, saw there was hay in the manger and water in his bucket, then went towards the house.

He was suddenly glad that Vania was

there and he knew she would be waiting to hear what had happened, and although it was only dismal news, he wanted to share it with somebody.

He found himself running up the steps to the front door, then as he entered he thought that something was different.

He realised it was because the Hall looked much cleaner and there was a large bowl of spring flowers on the table at the bottom of the stairs just where his mother had always placed them.

"And what have you done?" Tyson enquired.

"I did the flowers for you and entirely by my own cleverness I found the cupboard and now I have washed all the china. You see the difference it makes."

"It does indeed," he answered. "I cannot think why I did not realise all those things were missing. I just thought the room looked empty and depressing."

"How like a man!" Vania exclaimed.

Then as if she remembered why he had gone to Canterbury, she asked:

"Have you any news?"

"Yes, but it's not very constructive."

"What did Mr Chessington tell you?"

"Only that my father drew all his fortune out of the Bank which he had a hunch was going to crash, and which in fact did. But there is no record of any sort to tell us where he put his money."

Vania looked at him wide-eyed.

"How extraordinary! Are you saying that he knew instinctively that the Bank was unsound?"

"My father had a perception that was almost clairvoyant about such things," Tyson explained.

"But if he is your father, the chances are that you have it too," Vania suggested.

Tyson looked at her in surprise.

"Do you think such gifts are handed down from one person to another?"

"Why not?" she asked. "If your father was clever enough to remove his money before he lost it all, you ought to be clever enough to know where he has hidden it."

Tyson smiled.

"I wish it was as easy as that," he said. "I have been racking my brains as to where I could look, but my Solicitor has, in fact, made enquiries of all the local Banks and drawn a complete blank."

"Then if the money is not in a Bank where is it likely to be?" Vania asked.

"Here in the house," Tyson replied, "but that has also been searched from, I am told, attic to cellars."

"By strangers from outside!" Vania said. "Of course they would not find it. Your father would have hidden it very cleverly. It is you who must find out where it is."

"It sounds easy," Tyson replied, "but quite frankly, I have no idea where to start looking."

"You must think. I am certain you will come up with an answer," Vania said.

She gave a little cry.

"But I am forgetting — you must be hungry and tired after such a long ride! Hawkins has gone to prepare tea. I said we would have it in the little room where I am sure your mother had tea, and perhaps breakfast because it gets the sun."

"How did you know that?" Tyson asked.

"Oh, I am perceptive too," Vania replied lightly, "and very perceptive about this lovely, attractive house. I have found one treasure — all those lovely china pieces. Why should I not be able to find other things as well?"

"I hope you do!" Tyson said in all seriousness.

She put her head on one side before she said:

"Of course . . . it will take time."

"Now I see what you are aiming at!" he exclaimed. "What you are saying is that I can hardly turn you out when you are busy at trying to find perceptively where my fortune is hidden!"

"Exactly!" Vania agreed. "And after I have gone, if you did not find it yourself you would always be haunted by the fact that you might have lost it entirely by being so cruel and unkind to me."

"Your reasoning is illogical and quite preposterous!" Tyson announced.

At the same time he was smiling.

They went to the small Morning-Room where Hawkins was laying the tea.

"I see you have been working very hard, Hawkins," Tyson said, "and the results are better than I could possibly have anticipated."

The man smiled his appreciation, then when he withdrew from the room, Tyson said:

"Hawkins is another person with whom I shall have to have a serious talk, and I have a feeling, although I may be wrong, that he is going to be as reluctant as you are to leave."

"He has no intention of leaving any more than I have!" Vania replied. "We talked it over this afternoon, and we have both agreed, Hawkins and I, that we have to get things what you might call 'ship-shape'."

"Since you have decided everything

without me," Tyson said, "I suppose the mere fact that I own the house is of no consideration."

"Hawkins and I both want to do what is best for you and Revel Royal," Vania said, as if he was being rather obtuse and stupid. "Personally, I think it is the most adorable, attractive place I have ever seen in my whole life, and like Hawkins I want to see it looking clean and beautiful. Then we can start worrying about what comes next."

"You are twisting me," Tyson said, " 'round your little finger' — that is the right expression I think, and quite frankly, I do not like it. I have always been very self-sufficient and what is more, I have always been in command."

"I know that," Vania said. "It is written all over you, but you no longer have platoons of soldiers to order about. You only have me, and Hawkins and the Briggses! Think how helpless you would be if you lost half your attacking force. It could result in complete defeat!"

"I am not going to be drawn into a wordy duel," Tyson said.

"Too proud?" Vania teased.

"Too cautious," he replied, "but shall I add that I am very glad you love my house as I love it."

"And if it loves you," Vania said, "which I am sure it does, then I think it will show you the way to discover what it is hiding."

"How can we be sure that it is hiding anything?" Tyson asked.

"What you need is faith and hope," Vania said briskly, "and as you are sounding depressed you must have a slice of chocolate cake which Mrs Briggs has made for you. She told me it was your favorite when you were a boy and she always made it for you if ever you had been punished because it cheered you up."

"Good Heavens, I had forgotten that!" Tyson exclaimed. "I remember now. When I was sent to bed without any supper for some terrible misdeed, Mrs Briggs would always creep up the stairs and slip a huge slice of cake in through my bedroom door.

" 'Eat it quickly, Master Tyson!' she would say, 'and don't leave any incriminating crumbs about!' "

Vania laughed.

"She is a wonderful old woman, and she is full of stories about what you did when you were a little boy and how kind and sweet your mother was. Everybody loved her, Mrs Briggs told me, and the villagers all cried their eyes out when she died."

Vania's voice was very soft and Tyson for

the moment found it difficult to speak.

He had deliberately not talked of his mother since his return home for the simple reason that he felt it would be hard to bear the pain of hearing how she had died and knowing he had not been able to be there with her.

Now he knew that he would never tell Vania of the slur that had been cast upon his mother's name by his relatives.

He could fill in so much that Mr Chessington had not said — first of the sudden demand when his father died that his uncle must have made for documents to prove their marriage.

Perhaps his Uncle George had always suspected that because his mother had been under age when she and his father had run away, they had been unable to get married and therefore had pretended to be legally man and wife.

It was just the sort of sneaking, underhand idea that would fester in his uncle's mind and he would have jumped at an opportunity to prove a contention which no-one else would have credited for a moment.

So, when no certificate of marriage could be found, he had been able to announce himself heir presumptive to the Barony and then became the 6th Lord Wellingdale when, as Tyson knew, the position was his by right of birth.

He thought at that moment he was not really concerned with himself, but only in proving that his mother was as good and pure as in his heart he knew her to be.

Perhaps Vania was right — somewhere in this dilapidated, crumbling house there were papers with which he could confront his uncle and which would force from him an apology which Tyson would ring in his ears like a paean of triumph.

"I *have* to find my father's hiding-place," he told himself. "I have to!"

He did not speak aloud, and yet he felt almost as if he shouted the words for all to hear them.

Then he looked to find Vania watching him.

"You will win," she said quietly, almost as if she knew what he was thinking, "of course you will win! How could Perseus fail?"

Chapter 4

Vania ran down the stairs still buttoning her blouse.

She realised she was late, for she had dozed off again after Mrs Briggs had called her.

It was, she thought, not surprising that she was tired, as they had been late last night and working up to the very moment before they went to bed.

Tyson had decided, and she had agreed, that the best place to look for the money his father had hidden was in the Library.

"If I was concealing something in this house," he said, "I should put it behind the books or perhaps there is a cupboard, which I do not remember, like the one in the Salon."

"We will take the books down one by one and see if there is anything behind them," Vania said.

Before they started Tyson had insisted

that she ask Mrs Briggs if she could borrow one of her aprons.

"You are worrying about my gown again," Vania said with a smile.

"It is a very pretty one," Tyson replied, "and I would hate you to ruin it on my account."

She wanted to ask him if he thought she was pretty too, but she felt too shy to do so, even though she told herself almost resentfully it would not hurt him to pay her a compliment occasionally.

She could not help feeling that any other man, even the nauseating Sir Neville, would be flattering her and saying complimentary things which would make her blush.

Tyson merely looked at her with his grey eyes and she was not certain whether the expression in them was admiring or critical.

Then she told herself severely she was being selfish.

Of course he was too preoccupied with his own troubles to notice a mere woman, however pretty she might be.

Nevertheless, before she went downstairs, for the simple meal they ate at an early hour because Mrs Briggs got tired in the evenings, she took a lot of trouble over her appearance.

Her gown had been a very expensive one

and she was well aware that her aunt had chosen it to fascinate the man she was to marry and to wear at the parties which would be given for them in London once their engagement was announced.

In consequence Vania had decided she hated it and all the other gowns that had been bought for the same purpose.

But when she saw it hanging in the wardrobe in the bedroom which had belonged to Tyson's mother, she knew that it would become her and make her look like a Princess out of a fairy-tale.

She had indeed, as she went downstairs, thought she was a little overdressed. Then she asked herself for whom was she keeping her gowns?

Doubtless when Tyson sent her away she would be somewhere where nobody would notice what she wore.

The thought was depressing but she soon forgot it in the excitement of what she called their 'treasure-hunt'.

It was certainly a very dirty one.

The dust on the books after years of neglect made their hands, their clothes and even their faces dirty before they had finished.

It was impossible to search the whole Library in one evening, but on Tyson's instructions they did it systematically, moving along shelf after shelf, looking behind the books, trying the sides to see if there was a hinge so that the whole bookcase could swing open to reveal a hiding-place behind it! But all without any result.

The only consolation was that after they had been working for nearly three hours it had occurred to Vania to say:

"We have been so intent on looking for the treasure that we have not examined the books themselves. I am certain some of them must be quite valuable."

"That is certainly an idea," Tyson conceded, "and I might ask an expert from London to come down and examine them, but as you well know, that would cost money."

Vania did not reply. She merely redoubled her efforts in pulling the books from the shelves, only to discover nothing but dust and more dust.

They laughed at each other's appearance before finally they had gone up the stairs side by side each holding a candle.

Tyson opened the door of his mother's room.

"I like to think of you sleeping here," he said, "and I hope now you feel safe and are no longer afraid."

"I have a . . . feeling that your mother is . . . protecting me," Vania said in a low voice.

She thought as she spoke, that he might think it presumptuous of her to say such a thing, but he only replied seriously:

"I am sure she is. My mother always wanted to help anyone who was unhappy or in any difficulty."

"Then I am sure she will help you," Vania said quickly. "Goodnight, Tyson."

"Goodnight, Vania!"

He shut the door and she heard him go into the Master Bedroom next door.

She listened to him moving about, then with a little sigh, because she was very tired, she began to undress. . . .

Now as Vania burst into the Morning-Room she saw as she expected, that Tyson had finished his breakfast and was just rising to his feet as she entered.

"I am so sorry I am late," she said breathlessly. "I overslept and, do you know, I had the most extraordinary dream last night . . . ?"

"One moment," Tyson interrupted. "I will just tell Briggs you are down. I sent your breakfast away to keep hot."

He walked to the door as he spoke and

Vania heard him calling Briggs from the passage.

She sat down at the table, helped herself to a piece of toast and spread on it the golden-yellow Jersey butter which Hawkins had purchased from a neighbouring farm.

She thought how much more exciting it would be if Tyson could eat butter from one of his own farms and have his own cattle in the meadows which lay on each side of the twisting stream which ran through the estate.

Tyson came back into the room to say:

"Your breakfast is just coming and I see you have put on your riding-habit."

"You said last night that you wanted to ride first thing this morning."

"I thought it would be a good idea to take our exercise before we became too intent on our exploration inside the house."

He looked at her and smiled.

"I am glad you have washed your face. I thought last night after we had finished that we both looked like a rather disreputable pair of chimney-sweeps!"

"That is what I thought when I looked at myself in the mirror," Vania replied, "except that I was grey instead of being black."

"That reminds me," Tyson said, "I suppose I ought to get a chimney-sweep in before we attempt to light a fire in any of the rooms. I am quite certain the starlings have built their nests in them over the years, and we would be smoked out."

"How very practical!" Vania exclaimed. "That is something I should never have thought of."

"I do not suppose you have ever had to worry your head over such mundane matters," Tyson replied dryly.

Old Briggs came into the room carrying a plate over which Mrs Briggs had put another upside-down to keep the eggs and bacon it contained, warm.

He set it down in front of Vania.

"Thank you so much," she said. "I am sorry to be such a nuisance, but at home we always had breakfast-dishes with a lighted wick underneath them, so that if I was late, everything kept warm."

She spoke without thinking particularly of what she was saying, and because she was hungry started to eat.

A moment or two later she realised that Briggs was still standing by her side and his hand had gone up with his fingers on his forehead.

"Now I remembers!" he said. "You'll

think, Mr Tyson, that my head's like a sieve, an' so it is."

Tyson looked at him in surprise.

"What are you talking about?"

"I clean forgot th' silver — I did really!" the old man went on. "I put it away where I thought it'd be safe after the Master died, and I've grown so used to bein' without it I've never given it 'nother thought 'til now."

"The silver?" Tyson questioned. "I suppose I should have noticed that there should be a great deal more of it. But now you mention it, what has happened to the candelabra and the silver entrée dishes which we always used in the past?"

"That's just wot I were atelling you, Master Tyson," Briggs replied. "They be in th' cellar. I locked it all away where I knew no burglars'd ever find it."

Vania looked up at Tyson with a light in her eyes.

"It is not in the cellar," he said in a low voice, as he did not wish to upset Briggs, "for I looked in there yesterday."

Briggs however, who was walking towards the door, turned back to say:

"That's 'cause you didn't look in th' new cellar, Master Tyson."

"The new cellar?" Tyson questioned.

"Soon after you went away to th' war,"

Briggs answered, "the Master says to me, he says: 'Wine is going to get difficult to buy, Briggs, while we are fighting the French, and it will certainly not get any cheaper. We will get in a good store for Master Tyson when he comes home. He will want to drink to England's victorious Army when they have defeated Bonaparte'."

"A good store!" Tyson repeated almost beneath his breath.

"We all worked hard preparing for it," Briggs went on. "Come along now, Master Tyson, an' I'll show it to you. I've got th' key in th' Pantry."

The old man shuffled out. Vania took another piece of bacon, put it into her mouth and sprang to her feet.

"A treasure-trove!" she exclaimed. "And perhaps your father also used the cellar as a hiding-place."

Tyson did not answer, but she was sure he was as excited as she was as they followed Briggs down the passage.

They waited while with maddening slowness he searched in several drawers in the Pantry before finally at the back of one of them he found a large key.

Then they set off again, the old butler leading the way down the flagged passage off which there were steep stone stairs which led down to the cellars under the house.

There was some delay while they had to find a candle and light it. Then with Vania holding onto Tyson's hand for fear of slipping on the narrow steps, they went deeper and deeper into what seemed to be the bowels of the earth.

The cellar was very cold and low-ceilinged and as Tyson had seen when he had inspected it before, there was nothing there but some empty wine-racks rotting with age and a dozen large wooden barrels.

These had once contained the ale which the servants in his father's time drank with their meals.

This was the cellar he thought that he remembered, but Briggs walked on to the far end of it.

Here, although Tyson had not noticed it, was a door behind some wooden boxes.

Briggs put the key he carried in the lock, but it had grown so rusty through lack of use that he could not turn it.

"Let me try," Tyson suggested.

Handing the old man the candlestick, he managed by using both his hands, to turn the key.

He pulled the door open and as the candle-light revealed what appeared to be a large cavern with a flagged floor, he saw almost incredulously on both sides of it, rack upon rack filled with bottles of wine!

"It took a long time to get it just as th' Master wanted," Briggs said, "and he said as how the wine'd improve with keeping."

"It will have done that," Tyson said.

Vania clapped her hands together.

"A whole cellar of wine which you never knew existed!" she cried excitedly. "How wonderful! I wondered if you minded drinking only water for dinner."

Tyson looked around him.

"I can hardly believe it!" he exclaimed beneath his breath.

"And here be th' silver, Master Tyson," Briggs called.

He had walked almost to the end of the cavern where the racks ended, and following him, Vania and Tyson saw there was a large pile of objects all wrapped in green baize.

Tyson picked up one that was on the top and pulled off its baize covering. Vania saw a large comfit-dish tarnished black but obviously of exquisite workmanship.

"I remember this," Tyson said. "It was always on the table at parties and Briggs used to give me some of the bon-bons it contained the next day."

"Fancy you remembering that now!" the

old man said. "But you was always acoming to th' Pantry when you was a little 'un asking for something fancy to eat."

"And you would give me not only bon-bons but grapes and sometimes if I had been very good, a ripe peach."

Vania was crouching down pulling the green baize away from the objects on the floor to see what they were.

"Here are the entrée dishes," she exclaimed, "and I am quite sure these are the ones that you used for breakfast with a wick which keeps the food hot."

"We will take them upstairs," Tyson said, "but I suppose you realise there will be a lot of work required in cleaning them?"

"I know exactly what you are inferring," Vania replied, "and because owing to my simple remark you have found enough wine in which to drown your sorrows, you will have to help me."

She smiled at him as she spoke and Tyson smiled back.

It struck her suddenly that they were behaving rather like husband and wife setting up house together, and almost as if the same thought had occurred to Tyson, he said hastily:

"I will tell Hawkins to bring these things up for us, but now our horses are waiting."

"Perhaps we should offer them a bottle of wine as a token of apology," Vania teased. "They might enjoy it as much as you."

"I am not wasting my good wine on man or beast who would not really appreciate it," Tyson said firmly.

He led the way back to the other cellar and when they had passed through the door, he locked it and put the key in his pocket.

Only when they had reached the top of the cellar stairs did he say:

"You had better finish your breakfast."

"I am too excited to want to eat or drink," Vania said. "I told you I would help you find your treasures and this is Number Two on the list."

Tyson looked at her enquiringly, then she said:

"Have you forgotten the china? You said yourself you did not remember the cupboard being there."

"You are quite right," he agreed, "and in case you think I am being ungrateful, thank you!"

Vania ran into the Morning-Room to pick up her riding-hat and the jacket of her habit which she had left on a chair before she began her breakfast.

She put them on, thinking as she gave herself a quick glance in the gilt-framed mirror over the mantelpiece that the sapphire blue of her expensive habit was very becoming, as was the riding-hat with its gauze veil floating behind it.

"I am helping him," she told her reflection. "He is beginning to think I am useful."

However, she knew Tyson disliked being kept waiting, so she hurried out into the Hall where he handed her a thin riding-whip and her gloves.

She saw as he walked ahead of her down the steps where Hawkins was waiting with the two horses that his riding-clothes were old, and she had learnt from Mrs Briggs that they had belonged to his father.

Even so she thought that no man could look more handsome or more at home on a horse.

There was something about him that was very impressive, Vania told herself when a few minutes later they were riding over the bridge that spanned the lake.

She thought too there was something raffishly attractive about the way he wore his tall hat on the side of his dark head.

"I will race you!" she said impulsively. "My lungs are still full of dust from those books last night."

As she spoke they started thundering over the green turf.

She knew Salamanca would beat Vittoria but there was a wild elation in going so quickly and pitting her skill against a man who she knew would always be victorious in anything he undertook.

When they had galloped for over a mile, they drew in their horses and Vania said:

"I feel better after that! Oh, Tyson, was it not exciting to find all that lovely wine? Think how 'foxed' you will be able to get without it costing you a penny!"

"I have no intention of getting foxed," Tyson replied, "but it is certainly an unexpected pleasure to find I own something so luxurious."

"This is only the beginning," Vania said. "You mark my words, the house is like an Aladdin's Cave and we have only to find the magic word to make it reveal all its secrets."

"I hope you are right."

"I know I am right!" Vania said positively, "and just for once be gracious and say you are glad I am with you. If I had not said the 'magic word' to Briggs, the wine and the silver would have stayed there undiscovered. He might even have died and you would never have known of its existence."

"I have already said thank you," Tyson answered, but she saw that his eyes were twinkling.

"At times I detest your stiff-lipped British reserve," Vania complained, "and wish you were an ardent Frenchman saying delightful things that would make my heart beat quicker."

"A Frenchman?" Tyson queried. "Why not Sir Neville Blakely?"

"I really do detest you!" Vania retorted. "Now you have frightened me and I shall expect to see him pop over a fence, or come stalking me from between the trees!"

She touched Vittoria with her whip as she spoke and rode off at a gallop. Tyson following her thought it would be difficult to find a woman who rode better or looked more lovely.

He knew that if he was honest he would admit that he liked having Vania with him, and was well aware that he would feel very depressed if he was alone.

He had grown used to the company of men, of always having somebody to talk to and having to deal with dozens of problems a day that only he could solve.

He realised that to be by himself at Revel Royal with its fallen ceilings, its crumbling walls, its dust and dilapidation, would have driven him nearly to despair.

But with Vania, her enthusiasm, her child-like excitement, her provocative remarks, made everything seem fun and his troubles became part of the adventure story that she believed it to be.

She looked back to see if he was following and he had a quick glimpse of her huge eyes, her small straight nose and smiling lips.

"She is lovely! Far too lovely for any man's peace of mind," Tyson told himself, "and the sooner I make some plans for her future the better!"

Because it was such a fine morning they rode further than Tyson had intended and it was nearly noon when they returned to Revel Royal.

Hawkins was waiting to take their horses to the stables, and Vania pulling off her riding-hat walked into the Salon.

Tyson followed her.

"I was just thinking," she said, "that I should water the flowers before we start to do anything else."

"I believe you are dreading the moment when we start again on the Library," Tyson said. "I must admit it is not a task I particularly fancy."

"We could try one of the other rooms," Vania suggested.

"That would be a haphazard way of doing things," he replied.

"Now you are back to being a Commander-in-Chief," she teased. "The Army must advance in its accepted formation as laid down by the Duke of Marlborough, or would you prefer to recall what happened at Agincourt?"

"You are deliberately provoking me," Tyson said. "I have already warned you that one day you will go too far."

She put her head on one side in a manner which secretly he found rather fascinating before she replied:

"You are a civilian now, and I am doing my best to make you forget all that 'spit and polish' which is quite unnecessary in peacetime."

Tyson nearly remarked that there had not been much spit and polish about the Army which had fought its way over the Pyrenees, half-forgotten by those who lived in comfort in England, or the troops that finally defeated Soult's forces at the Battle of Toulouse.

But he knew that to say such things would merely make him sound pompous as Vania accused him of being. Instead he said:

"All right, I give in! You choose where we start to search next."

As he spoke he suddenly to his surprise heard voices in the Hall.

Vania heard them too. She looked at him

and they both had the same thought.

"You must not be found here!" Tyson said quickly. "Go out through the window."

"I might be seen," Vania whispered. "I have a better idea."

As she spoke, she ran across the room to the fireplace, pulled open the door of the cupboard in the panelling where she had found the china ornaments and slipped inside.

As she did so, Tyson saw she had left her riding-hat on a chair and picking it up, he dropped it behind the sofa.

He heard the cupboard close as the door of the Salon opened.

"The Honourable Manfred Dale, Master Tyson!" old Briggs announced in a quavering voice.

Tyson stiffened and as he did so, a man came into the room who was so flamboyantly attired, so very much a 'Tulip of Fashion', that for a moment he did not recognise him.

It was, in fact, over fourteen years since he had last seen his cousin, and as then he had been little more than a boy and an obnoxious one at that, it was hardly surprising that in this elegant fashion-plate figure it was hard to recognise Manfred.

It was obvious that the newcomer thought

that Tyson had altered too; for he stood looking at him for a moment, before he drawled:

"It *is* Tyson, I suppose? Although I swear it would have been darned hard for me to know you, had we met elsewhere."

"I might say the same," Tyson replied. "What do you want?"

He spoke sharply and Manfred laughed in an affected manner.

"How like you! How very like you, my dear cousin, which I suppose I must call you — even though you were born on the wrong side of the blanket!"

"I did not invite you here," Tyson said abruptly, "and I therefore have no compunction in asking your reason for calling on me. I can hardly believe it is in my interest."

"Very perceptive!" Manfred sneered. "Am I invited to sit down? I could do with some refreshment."

"I have no intention of offering you anything," Tyson replied. "Kindly acquaint me with your reason for calling then leave as quickly as possible."

"So that is your attitude! I imagined you would show some sportsmanship — let the best man win and all that sort of thing."

"Your father's behaviour is something I

do not wish to discuss."

"My dear cousin, that attitude is, if I may say so, to be expected. At the same time if your Solicitors could have shown any proof that your father and mother were united in matrimony, then of course my father would not have pressed his claim."

"He would have been unable to do so," Tyson said grimly.

Manfred Dale had seated himself in a comfortable armchair.

"You are fortunate that your mother left you this house, but it certainly needs money spent on it."

"You are not here to discuss my house, I presume?" Tyson said. "Why have you come?"

"Blunt to the point of rudeness!" Manfred remarked, "but I suppose I should have expected nothing else."

Tyson did not reply. He merely waited with a grim look on his face.

He had moved to stand with his back to the empty fireplace and although his cousin's snowy white cravat was tied in the intricate style affected by the Bucks of St James's, his champagne-coloured pantaloons fitted closely and his exquisitely fit tailcoat was without a wrinkle, Tyson in his father's old riding-kit looked double the man.

There were only two years between the cousins, but years of war and the authority he had gained in the field of battle had given Tyson a maturity which was completely lacking in the languid figure of the Dandy who faced him.

As if the contrast between them gradually percolated into Manfred's mind, the expression in his eyes seemed to change and he said surlily:

"I came to see if you could help me."

"Help you?" Tyson queried in surprise.

"I suppose you have heard of the crime that has taken place in the village which adjoins your property?"

"Crime? What crime?"

"When did you get back?" Manfred asked. "I suspected you might be here, but the people at the Inn said they had not seen you."

"I arrived from Dover on Tuesday," Tyson said, "not that it is any business of yours."

"Tuesday . . ." Manfred repeated. "Then I fancy you cannot assist me."

"In what way did you think I might?" Tyson enquired.

"On Tuesday night a Mr and Mrs Charlwood were unfortunately compelled because their horse had cast a shoe, to stay the night in the Posting Inn at Little Fenwick."

Tyson made no movement. He only listened with his eyes on his cousin's face.

"They were accompanied by their niece," Manfred went on, "Evangeline Charlwood, to whom when they reached London I had intended to announce my engagement."

"You are to be married?" Tyson said. "I must congratulate you!"

"I would, of course, appreciate your congratulations more," Manfred replied, "if when staying in what I am sure you think of as 'your village' the young lady in question had not disappeared."

"Disappeared?" Tyson exclaimed. "How could she have done that?"

"That is what I want to know," Manfred answered. "When I was informed of what had happened I posted here from London immediately, only to find that she had vanished without leaving a clue behind her."

"How is that possible?"

"That is what I want to find out."

"There must be someone who has some idea of what happened."

"No-one," Manfred replied firmly.

Tyson appeared to be thinking for a moment. Then he said:

"Perhaps, although of course I only sug-

140

gest it as a possibility, she might have eloped with somebody else?"

"Dammit, that is exactly what the people in the Inn tried to tell me! But her uncle, a very reliable man, assures me that she knew very few men with the exception of a fortune-hunter called Sir Neville Blakely who was found on the floor of her bedroom assaulted, so he said, by an unknown assailant whose face he did not see."

Tyson sighed.

"It seems a very complicated tale. Have you any reason to think the lady in question did not wish to marry you?"

"Of course she wants to marry me!" Manfred snapped. "I am her entry into a Social World which she had not so far encountered, and, of course, eventually . . ."

He paused as if he remembered to whom he was speaking.

"Eventually," Tyson finished, "she would become, on your father's death, Lady Wellingdale."

"Yes, if you want to put it so bluntly," Manfred agreed.

"And you really wish to marry her?"

"Of course I wish to," Manfred snapped. "She is an heiress, and a very considerable one!"

"I am beginning to see daylight!"

"It has taken some time to percolate your brain!" he sneered. "The marriage has been arranged by my father and this girl's uncle to the satisfaction of both."

"And to yours? Why should you need an heiress? My grandfather was a very rich man."

"Does one ever have enough money?" Manfred asked languidly. "As it happens, I have under my protection a very attractive little 'nightingale' from Covent Garden who has the most extravagant taste in diamonds!"

"Then of course you must find your heiress with all possible speed," Tyson said sarcastically.

"That is what I intend to do," Manfred replied. "I thought perhaps you might have heard something locally which would put me on the right track, but I can see I was mistaken."

He rose slowly to his feet.

"If I could help you," Tyson said, "you may be sure I would not do so."

"Of course! Bastard by birth, and bastard by nature!" Manfred drawled. "Well, it is unlikely that our paths will cross in the future."

"You need not be too sure of that," Tyson warned, "and you can tell your father that I have every intention of challenging his right to the title and to the estates."

Manfred laughed and it was not a pleasant sound.

"They say the British soldier never knows when he is beaten," he sneered. "But keep your optimism: you do not seem to have much else!"

He walked towards the door.

"Goodbye, my most inhospitable and illegitimate cousin. I shall not invite you to my wedding. A family skeleton should never leave the cupboard."

He went from the room as he spoke but Tyson did not move.

Slowly with an effort he unclenched his hands.

It was only years of practising self-control which had prevented him from striking his cousin, and though it would have given him intense satisfaction to do so he knew it would have been undignified and it would also have prolonged the stay of a very un-welcome visitor.

He stood until he heard the sound of wheels moving away from the front door. Then as if someone else had been listening for them too the door of the cupboard behind him opened.

He turned and saw that Vania's large eyes

seemed almost to fill her face.

She was very pale and though her lips moved, it seemed for a moment as if no sound would come from them.

"So your name is Evangeline Charlwood!" Tyson remarked.

"And yours . . . is Tyson . . . Dale."

"I thought you knew that."

"N–no, I believed . . . because of the pictures that your name was Osborne."

"I would have explained if I had thought you had anything to do with my cousin."

"Now you see," she murmured hardly above a whisper, "what he is . . . like . . . why I could not . . . marry him!"

"No, of course not."

Their eyes met, and as they looked at each other it seemed as if they spoke without words. Then Tyson turned and walked away from her across the room to the window.

He stood staring out with unseeing eyes and after what seemed to be a long silence Vania said in a frightened voice:

"Y–you will not . . . send me . . . away?"

"You know that you cannot stay here."

"Why . . . not?"

"Because now I know who you are, I am obliged to communicate your whereabouts to your uncle."

"Why? Why? You know that if you do so he will . . . force me to marry that . . . beastly cousin of . . . yours."

Vania spoke violently, then she moved to stand beside Tyson at the window.

"Why did he speak to you like that?" she asked. "Why did he call you those horrible names?"

"My father ran away with my mother because he loved her," Tyson explained. "She was under age and no-one knows where they were married. But they were married, I am convinced of it."

"But your uncle says they were not?"

"When my father died he asked for proof of the marriage," Tyson replied. "I was abroad fighting and the Solicitors could find no documents, no information of any sort, as to where the ceremony took place."

"So your uncle became Lord Wellingdale."

"My father was the elder son."

"I can . . . understand," Vania said, "how it . . . hurt you."

"It does not worry me what Manfred calls me," Tyson replied, "but I will clear my mother's name if it takes me my whole lifetime to do so."

Again he thought he was repeating the vow he had made to himself. Then he felt a small hand on his arm.

"We will do it. We will find the proof . . . together here in this house — I am sure of it!" an eager little voice said.

Tyson put his other hand over hers.

"Thank you, Vania, but it may take a long time and that is something you cannot afford to give me."

"I can and I will!" Vania retorted. "Are you really prepared to force me into marriage with that . . . drawling beast, who only wants my . . . money so that he can . . . spend it on some other . . . woman?"

"Are you really very rich?"

"Yes, very!"

"Then how can I keep you here?" he asked. "If it was discovered, you can imagine what everybody would say."

She did not speak and he went on:

"Not only your reputation would be ruined, but I should be sent to Australia in chains for abduction! It would also spoil everything that is lovely and young and untouched about you, and this is something I could not bear."

There was a note in his voice that made Vania look up at him enquiringly and as if he realised his hand was still on hers, Tyson moved.

"We have to discuss this very sensibly,"

he said firmly, "as we should have done already. I am trying to think of some feasible plan. In fact, I think I have one!"

"What is . . . it?" Vania asked in a whisper.

"It is that I should take you in a carriage which I expect I can hire in the village and put you down near your home. You can return to your uncle and say that you have been staying in various wayside Inns in an effort to avoid Sir Neville, which was why you left the *Dog and Duck*."

Tyson spoke crisply in the same voice, although Vania did not know it, that he had used when suggesting a deployment of his troops or a special plan of campaign to Wellington.

"It is a thin explanation," he finished. "I admit it is thin, but I think your uncle will be so glad to have you home that he will not ask too many questions."

Vania drew a deep breath.

"You have . . . forgotten . . . something."

"What is that?"

"That I have no . . . intention of going back to my . . . uncle."

"You have to!"

"And be forced into marriage with your cousin?"

She faced Tyson defiantly as she spoke and now he looked away from her. She knew without either of them saying anything that she had scored a telling point.

There was a long silence.

"You must have some other relations," Tyson remarked at length.

"Only elderly aunts who will do anything my uncle suggests and will think it a splendid thing for me to marry the future Lord Wellingdale."

"You must have cousins?"

"There are some, but I do not know them. Uncle Lionel never invited any of them to stay."

Tyson moved restlessly.

"You cannot be the only person in the world with no relatives, no friends, to whom you can turn in a situation like this."

"Perhaps I am unique," Vania said, "but it . . . happens to be the . . . truth."

"Then what are we to do?"

Tyson asked the question angrily, then as his eyes met Vania's they were both very still.

"Let me . . . stay," she pleaded almost beneath her breath.

"I have told you that is impossible."

"I could . . . suggest a way it would be . . . possible."

"How?"

"You . . . you could . . . marry me!"

Chapter 5

For a moment Tyson stared at Vania as if he thought he could not have heard her aright.

Then he said in a voice which sounded unexpectedly harsh:

"Do you know what you are saying?"

"You would . . . protect me . . . and I would be . . . safe with you."

He stood looking at her as if he still doubted his own hearing. Then he walked away to stand with his back to her, his hands on the mantelpiece.

"It is quite impossible."

"Why?"

"You know the answer to that."

"What is . . . it?"

Tyson did not reply and after a moment Vania said in a nervous little voice:

"It may have seemed . . . wrong to you that I should ask you . . . such a thing . . . but when I was . . . listening in the cupboard, I knew that I was not . . . exaggerating when I

149

told you that I would rather . . . die than marry your cousin."

"I will take you to your uncle," Tyson said. "I will explain to him the exceptional circumstances in which you found yourself and I will make him see sense."

He spoke forcefully as if he had no doubt that he could make Vania's uncle realise that it was impossible for her to marry a man whom she did not love or somebody so utterly alien to her in every way as Manfred Dale.

"He will . . . not listen . . . I know he will not . . . listen!" Vania said frantically. "If you send me back, he and my aunt will gradually . . . break down any . . . resistance I might . . . have."

"I will make him see sense."

"He may . . . pretend to do so while you are there, but when you have . . . gone he will get in touch with . . . Lord Wellingdale and however much I fight them, I shall be . . . forced into a marriage that I can only tell you would be like . . . going down into . . . hell itself!"

Vania spoke desperately as if she knew that Tyson was determined to do what he said.

As her words died away and he still did not turn round, there was a long silence until in a broken little voice that was infinitely pathetic he heard her say:

"P–perhaps . . . the real reason why you are saying . . . no . . . is because you do not . . . want me."

He turned round and now he saw she was only a few feet away from him and there was a stricken look in her eyes that he had never seen before.

For a moment they just looked at each other. Then he said:

"I have nothing to offer you."

"But if you had . . . would you . . . marry me?"

Their eyes met and it seemed as if Tyson's answer died on his lips. Then with an effort that was very obvious, he said:

"That is an hypothetical question and there is no point in my answering it."

"I . . . want to know."

"I have said the question does not arise. As you are well aware I can marry nobody, having not even a name to which I am legally entitled."

"You know that you will find . . . proof of that . . . here in this house, but by then it . . . may be too . . . late."

Tyson deliberately looked away from her pleading eyes.

"What I intend to do," he said, "is to hire

a carriage which will carry us to your uncle's house."

"You do not know where he lives."

"I will find out, or you will tell me because it is the only thing that we can do."

"Are you thinking of . . . me or of . . . yourself?"

Tyson's lips tightened, but he said quietly:

"Shall we say it is best for both of us?"

"Please . . . marry me."

Once again his eyes were on hers and she had the feeling that what he was saying in his heart was very different from the harsh words his lips spoke.

Then abruptly he said:

"I am leaving now. If it takes longer than I think it will, do not wait luncheon for me."

He walked across the room as he spoke, and as she gave a despairing little cry he shut the door sharply behind him.

Vania put her hands up to her face.

She did not cry, she merely felt as if in her abject despair she was past tears.

How could Tyson be so cruel as to take her back to her uncle when he knew that once she was in his house and under his jurisdiction, she would be forced into marriage, however much she might fight against it.

She had been so utterly miserable with her uncle and aunt that sometimes she thought that marriage to anyone would be preferable to living with people who did not want her and who disliked her because she was attractive and because she was so rich.

That was before she had met Manfred Dale.

She was not exaggerating when she told Tyson that she felt as if he was a reptile that not only frightened her, but made her creep every time he came near her.

She knew with some sensitive perception within herself that he was bad, positively evil, and it was impossible to bear the thought of his touching her let alone kissing her.

"I hate him!" she had cried the first time she met him, but her uncle had only laughed.

"All women are frightened of marriage," he said, "but later they grow to love their husbands."

"Love that man?" Vania replied. "Never! Never! I shall loathe and detest him until I die!"

"You ought to go down on your knees and thank God that anyone so important and who moves in the very best Society, should wish to marry you," her aunt said acidly.

Vania knew that her aunt was socially ambitious, and that the thought that through her husband they might enter what was known as the 'Beau Monde' was an enticement to which anything could be sacrificed including herself.

She had known when she was in the cupboard listening to Manfred Dale's drawling, affected voice, that the difference between him and Tyson was in her own mind, the difference between God and the Devil.

It was then she had known how deeply she already loved Tyson, and that she had in fact, loved him from the moment he had saved her from Sir Neville Blakely and brought her back in the moonlight to this enchanted house.

"I love him! I think I have always loved him because he has been there in my heart even before I saw him," she told herself. "He is just the sort of man I . . . dreamt I would meet one day."

She knew that every moment she had been at Revel Royal had been a joy that had deepened and grown more exciting minute by minute simply because Tyson was there.

To ride with him, to search for the treasure, to tease him and to hear his deep voice speaking her name was a magic that she had believed existed somewhere in the world, but which she had never found.

Now, when she held it in her hands, it was being taken from her.

"How can he be so . . . cruel? How can he make me . . . suffer like this?" she asked herself.

She thought perhaps she might run away again, but where could she go? And how, unless she walked or borrowed Vittoria, could she convey herself from one place to another?"

"Tyson . . . Tyson!" she called in her heart.

Then because she felt as though she was beating herself against an unyielding wall, she flung herself, face downwards on the sofa, hiding her eyes in one of the faded silk cushions. . . .

Riding Salamanca up the drive towards the village Tyson could only hear a rather frightened little voice saying:

"You . . . could . . . marry me."

It was an idea which he was well aware had already been in his own mind, although he had brushed it aside.

He had told himself he was crazy to think that he could ever be married or even think of a woman until he could prove that he was entitled to the name he had always borne and by some miracle find his father's fortune.

Although Vania, by turning their treasure-hunt into a game, had aroused an optimism that he felt was unjustified, some indomitable part of Tyson was convinced he would eventually be victorious.

He could not believe that his uncle's green and intrinsic wickedness could 'flourish like a green bay-tree' indefinitely.

Sooner or later he must be confronted with what Tyson knew was the truth. Then his father and mother would have restored to them the respect to which they had always been entitled.

Tyson had a number of relatives, although having been abroad he had not seen them for many years. But he had no intention of getting in touch with any of them.

He was certain they would have accepted his uncle's claim to the title and wouldn't wish to quarrel with him.

He could not really blame them for being what he thought of as 'chicken-hearted' for the simple reason that his father was dead while his uncle was very much alive.

What was more, although many of them were doubtless in touch with Manfred, they had no idea what he, Tyson, was like, or if he had any claim on their loyalty.

'I am alone in this,' he thought, 'and alone I have to win the battle. But now there is Vania!'

Her voice seemed to echo in his ears and he told himself he was like St Anthony being tempted to the point where it was almost impossible to withstand the allurements of what was offered.

Of course he wanted Vania, he thought, as Salamanca carried him through the lodge-gates out into the dusty road which led to the village.

No man with blood in his veins could resist those large pleading eyes, that flower-like face, that small exquisite figure.

It was not only her looks. He knew that she had shown unusual courage in fighting against being married to a man she disliked.

She had also been brave enough to leave the Inn with a perfect stranger just because, instinctively, she trusted him.

He found her optimism, her excitement, her faith that he would finally be victorious irresistible.

"But I have nothing to offer her, nothing!" he said to himself, dully.

And that he knew was like the tolling of a funeral-bell and there was no appeal against it.

He approached the *Dog and Duck* cautiously just in case his cousin Manfred had not yet left the village.

Skirting the green he peered inside the yard to see if there was any sign of the very smart black and yellow Phaeton in which Manfred had driven away from the front door of Revel Royal.

There were, however, only a few gigs belonging to local farmers who had dropped into the *Dog and Duck* for a drink, and standing on its shafts was an old-fashioned closed carriage which Tyson suspected was the only vehicle that would be for hire in the village.

He dismounted from Salamanca and as he did so, an ostler came up to take the horse's bridle.

"Good-day to ye, Sir. Shall Oi put 'e in the stable for ye?" he asked.

"I wish to see the Proprietor. I believe his name is Finch," Tyson said.

"Oi 'appen to know 'e be busy roight now, Sir."

"Then perhaps you could help me," Tyson said. "I want to hire a closed carriage with two horses."

The ostler, as he expected, looked towards the carriage in the centre of the courtyard.

"That be th' only closed carriage us 'as, Sir."

"Then it will have to do," Tyson replied. "Will you bring it to Revel Royal this afternoon?"

The ostler shook his head.

"The 'orses be out today, Sir. A gent-man wot be stayin' in th' Inn 'ave driven they off to Dover."

"Then when can I have them?"

"Termorrer, Sir."

"Then that will have to do," Tyson agreed.

"Ye be awantin' they at Revel Royal, did ye say?"

"That is right."

"Oi didn't know as anyone were aliving there."

"I have returned, as you see, from the wars."

"Then ye must be Mr Dale."

"I am."

"Nice to see ye, Sir. Oi've 'eard about ye ever since Oi be a boy, but Oi've been away too, servin' in th' Navy, Oi were for five year."

"Then I expect you are glad to be home," Tyson smiled.

"Oi were an' all," the ostler answered. "They said as Oi were too old to carry on a'ter Oi were wounded, an' Oi were thankful to get back 'ere alive."

"I think we all felt that."

Tyson glanced once again at the close carriage.

"Bring that vehicle with the horses to Revel Royal tomorrow."

"Ten of the clock suit ye, Sir?"

"Yes, that will do very well," Tyson replied.

He remounted Salamanca and rode out of the yard, having no idea that his conversation with the ostler had been watched from one of the windows.

The Honourable Manfred Dale leaning languidly against the Bar, said to the Proprietor:

"Cast your mind back, my man. See if you can remember who was here last Tuesday night."

Finch, who was not particularly quick-brained, scratched his head.

"There were a lady and gentleman whose horse had cast a shoe . . ."

"We have already discussed them," Manfred Dale interposed irritably. "Who else? Think of the men who were here."

"There were two gentlemen from the races, rather tipsy they got, having won a bit of money."

"Go on!"

"There were Farmer Lovegrove who lives th' other side of th' village."

"I am not interested in him," Manfred Dale snapped. "Who else? Think, man — think!"

Finch was obviously finding it hard to cast his mind back, then as he glanced out of the window, he exclaimed:

"There be one o' them, Sir. I 'members him now. Had a bottle of our best claret, he did, an' congratulated me on th' quality of it."

Manfred Dale turned his head slowly, then when he saw the man about whom the Proprietor was talking, his limp body seemed to stiffen and there was a very different expression on his face.

"You are quite certain that man was here on Tuesday night?" he asked.

"Yes, indeed, Sir. I 'members him well. To tell th' truth, I thinks he seemed too much o' a gentleman to be talking so pleasant-like to th' others in the Bar."

Manfred Dale did not reply.

He merely stood a little way back from the window watching Tyson until he rode away.

Then he said sharply to the Inn-Keeper:

"Go and find out what he said to your ostler, and be quick about it!"

As he spoke, he bent forward to look as far

as he could from the window of the Bar towards the gates onto the green.

He was hoping that as Tyson left he would not see his Phaeton returning and recognise it.

He had sent his groom to the next village to ask at the Inn there, if anyone had seen, last Tuesday night, a young lady either alone or accompanied, travelling with a large amount of luggage.

Tyson rode back slowly to Revel Royal.

With one part of him he wanted to see Vania again, knowing they had only twenty-four more hours together and that might have to last him a lifetime.

And yet every instinct within him shrank from encountering her pleading eyes, of hearing her lips ask questions to which he felt he had no answers.

Hawkins was waiting to take Salamanca and he knew by the dark expression on his master's face that something had happened to upset him.

He had seen him look like that when the battle was going badly, the Portuguese had served them some treacherous trick, or worse still, when they had found the bodies of their comrades who had been killed, robbed and often mutilated.

Hawkins, however, wisely said nothing, but merely took Salamanca back to the stables while Tyson walked in through the front door.

As he expected, Vania was waiting for him in the Salon, and as he entered the room, he tried to say in a normal voice:

"Is luncheon ready? I hope I am not late."

"What . . . have you . . . arranged?"

Vania's question was very low and tense.

"I have hired a carriage with two horses."

"When . . . when are they . . . coming?"

"Tomorrow. They were not available today."

He felt rather than saw the light that came into Vania's eyes.

At least she had twenty-four hours. At least there was some hope that she might persuade him not to send her away!

"All you have to do now," Tyson said, "is to tell me where I am to take you, but I think we would be wise to eat first."

"How can you . . . think of . . . food when you are treating me in such a . . . cruel . . . heartless manner?"

She was angry now which was, Tyson thought, better than when she had pleaded with him.

"Must we spend the next twenty-four hours quarrelling?" he asked. "I thought

163

perhaps we might go on with the treasure-hunt."

"Are you . . . saying that if we find your father's . . . money you will . . . marry me?"

"No, I am not saying that. There is something else I have to find."

"Proof of your mother and father's marriage?"

"Yes."

"And if you find both of those things . . . then will you . . . marry me?"

Their eyes met and although Tyson did not speak, Vania gave a little cry.

"You would! I know you would! You are too proud to tell me so, but I am . . . humble enough to say what is in my heart . . . I love . . . you!"

As she spoke she moved towards Tyson, but before she reached him, he turned away.

"For God's sake, Vania, do not say such things, or look at me like that," he pleaded. "I am a human being, although you may not think so!"

He walked out of the Salon and by the time Vania had followed him into the Hall he was half-way down the passage towards the Dining-Room having called sharply:

"Briggs! We are ready for luncheon!"

They spent the afternoon wandering

164

round the house, searching first one room, then another.

"I have already looked in my own bedroom," Tyson said.

"And I have searched every part of your mother's room," Vania replied. "Do you think your father would have gone up into the attics?"

"No, I am quite certain he would not have put anything there," Tyson answered. "There were servants sleeping there in the old days, quite a number of them. But the Gun-Room is a possibility."

They searched the Gun-Room, Tyson finding all sorts of things that brought back memories of his boyhood — the first small fishing-rod he ever used, the net for bringing in the larger trout which he and his father had fished for in the lake.

He found his first gun and in a corner of the room the toboggan he had thought about so often when he had been overseas and it had snowed on the mountains of Portugal.

Because it relieved the tension between them, he told Vania stories of his childhood and how happy he had always been at home.

"I cried all the way to School," he said, "and I used to cross off the days on a calendar until it was time to return for the holidays."

He sighed.

"Some boys preferred School to being at home, but I was certainly never one of them."

"I can understand that," Vania said, "but you must have enjoyed Oxford. Papa always said it was the happiest time of his life."

"I made a lot of friends there," Tyson said, "but when I went into the Army I lost touch with them, except for two who joined my Regiment at the same time as I did. They were both killed."

There was a sadness in his voice which made Vania say quickly:

"I am sorry."

"I suppose that is why I feel so alone now," Tyson said. "I have so few friends in this part of the world."

"You have . . . me," Vania replied without thinking.

As she spoke, she knew that she had brought back the tension between them that had been half-forgotten for the last few hours.

Tyson put the things they had taken from the shelves of the Gun-Room back in their places.

"There is nothing here," he said. "Shall we try somewhere else?"

He moved out of the room as he spoke and, following him, Vania thought it was as if he was always ahead of her and she could not catch up with him.

"After tomorrow I shall never see him again," she told herself.

She felt the pain of it was like a dagger thrust into her heart.

"How can I leave him? How can I bear to try to forget that we ever met?" she asked.

She knew the answer was that it would be impossible.

They had tea, then because the sun was still shining, they went out into the garden.

"When my father was alive there were ten gardeners," Tyson said as they walked over the weed-covered paths.

"Even though it is a wilderness it is still very beautiful!" Vania said softly, looking at where the cultured roses had gone 'wild' and the honeysuckle was rioting in an unrestrained manner.

"I see you had a herb-garden," she said.

They had passed through an old red brick wall and saw what had once been neat flower-beds edged with tiny box hedges.

"People used to come for miles to ask my mother for some particular remedy," Tyson replied.

"I wonder if there is . . . one for . . . heart-ache?"

"Must you torture me?"

"What do you . . . think you are . . . doing to . . . me?"

"I keep asking myself," he said in a low voice, "why I went to the *Dog and Duck* the first night I arrived? If I had stayed here in the house none of this would have happened."

"Are you . . . sorry you . . . met me?"

"You know that is not what I am thinking," Tyson said. "I am suffering just as you are — but there is nothing I can do about it."

"There is nothing you *will* do about it!" Vania corrected.

He was still for a moment, then he sat down on a stone seat which stood against one of the walls and Vania seated herself beside him.

"Look at this garden," Tyson said. "It is like my life: a hopeless mess! If one started to tidy it, one would not know where to begin. Do you think I could offer you that?"

"It would make me very . . . happy if you . . . did."

"Perhaps for a while but I would watch you gradually becoming disillusioned, gradually getting bored with the squalor, the poverty, the worry as to where the next meal was coming from."

She turned her face to look at him and he knew what she was thinking.

"Before you say it," he said harshly, "do you really believe I would touch a penny of your money unless I could equal it with my own?"

Vania did not reply.

She told herself it was what she knew he would feel and think, for how could he be anything but the exact opposite of his despicable cousin who only wished to marry her because she was rich?

"I would not . . . mind being . . . poor with . . . you," she said softly.

"That is what you think now," Tyson said. "Do you ever look in your mirror?"

"Of course!"

"And what do you see?"

"I see . . . myself."

"Then you must realise that self is very beautiful, but also a product of luxury."

He suddenly turned round to look at her and said in a voice she had never heard before:

"Oh, my precious, you are so exquisite, so different in every way from any other woman I have ever known before, that I could not spoil you, could not watch you becoming disillusioned or losing your beauty just because I have not enough money even to feed you properly."

"I love . . . you! Oh, Tyson, I love you with . . . all my . . . heart!"

"You are very young, you will get over it."

"As you . . . will?"

He looked away from her.

"I have never been in love until now," he said, "and I know I will never love anyone again as I love you."

"Please . . . Tyson . . . please let us be . . . adventurous! Let us . . . belong to each . . . other. Nothing . . . else in the world . . . matters."

"That is what I would like to believe, what I would like to say to you," Tyson replied, "but because I have some semblance of honour left, because I was brought up to believe that a man should revere the woman he loves and protect her, I find it impossible to behave like a cad."

"You are . . . sacrificing me to your . . . principles."

"Because you are you, and I am me," Tyson replied with a faint smile, "could you expect me to do anything else?"

"No . . . no!" Vania said. "You are behaving . . . exactly as in my heart I knew you would . . . But how can I live . . . without you

170

". . . even if you can live without me?"

"I have already asked myself that question," Tyson answered, "and I think we both know the answer. I would not spoil anything which is perfect, neither you nor my love for you."

He rose as he spoke and Vania knew by the expression on his face that he could bear no more.

In that moment her love for him suddenly matured and had new depths she did not even know existed.

Because she understood what he was feeling, because his suffering meant even more than her own, she slipped her hand into his and as she walked beside him she said in a very low voice:

"I understand . . . and I not only love . . . but worship you . . . because you are so wonderful and above all things a gentleman in every . . . meaning of the word."

His fingers tightened painfully on hers, but he did not speak.

In silence they walked back through the overgrown garden to the house.

Dinner was finished and Tyson poured himself out another glass of wine.

Tonight he had insisted on Vania drinking with him and she knew it was because he felt that the wine would perhaps alleviate some of their misery and the knowledge that the hours were passing and they would soon have to part.

Vania had still not told him where her uncle lived, but she knew when the moment came she would give Tyson the address simply because it would be impossible to hold out against him.

When she went up to change for dinner she had chosen her most elaborate and loveliest gown, one which her aunt had intended her to wear at the most important Ball to which she was invited when they reached London.

It was white, embroidered all over with tiny diamanté which sparkled and glittered as she moved, and as she came down the stairs Tyson thought she was like a star descending from the sky onto the earth below.

As if he knew that she would dress up for their last evening together, he too had searched among his father's clothes until he found the evening dress suit that gentlemen had worn during the festivities of the Armistice that had taken place in 1802.

In the knee-breeches, the silk stockings and the skilfully cut coat with long tails Tyson looked more magnificent and certainly more elegant than he had ever done before.

He had brushed his hair into the fashion-able coiffure of the moment and tied his white muslin cravat as cleverly as if, Vania thought, he had been taught by Beau Brummel himself.

"How magnificent you look!" she ex-claimed as she reached the centre of the stairs.

"And you look very lovely," he answered.

She curtsied at the compliment and he bowed, then they both laughed as if they were children playing a game.

They went into the Dining-Room to find that as usual Mrs Briggs had cooked them a very simple meal. Tyson had fetched the wine from the cellar and as he poured it into Vania's glass he said:

"I do not believe that anybody anywhere in England is enjoying better wine than we are at the moment."

As if he knew that this evening was a very special occasion old Briggs had cleaned one of the big candelabra that had been hidden in the cellar and it stood in the centre of the table with six lighted candles in it.

Now that dinner was over and they were alone Vania looked at Tyson sitting in a high-backed chair at the head of the table and said:

"One day I know you will give large parties in this room and your guests will listen with respect to what you have to say because you will be playing an important part in the County and its affairs."

"I think that is unlikely," Tyson replied. "Shall I tell you that wherever you are you will shine like the star you look tonight, and that men will be irresistibly attracted to you and I cannot bear to think of it."

"And if they are," Vania said, "I shall find they only wear one face, and that is yours! I shall only hear one voice, and that is yours! I can only think of one person, and that is you."

She spoke passionately and Tyson put out his hand, palm upwards towards her.

"I love you!" he said, "and you know I can never sit in this room without seeing you sitting where you are now and hearing your voice. You will haunt this house, and you will haunt me and nothing will ever be the same without you."

She put her hand in his and he knew the words which trembled on her lips, but because she loved him she did not say them.

"This has been a . . . dream," she said, "but I can never . . . awaken to how I was before. Even if you will not . . . have me, Tyson . . . I am yours! Yours completely . . . from now until . . . eternity."

His fingers closed slowly over hers. Then raising his glass, he said:

"I will not repeat what I have already said, my lovely one, but when I leave you I shall be a man without a heart, an empty shell, and I know that however long I live I shall never find love again."

They sat for a moment linked together by their hands, then Tyson released Vania, drank his glass of wine and they both rose and went from the Dining-Room along the dark passage which led to the Salon.

"Shall we have one more look and see if we can find the treasure?" Vania asked, as they reached the Hall.

Tyson shook his head.

"No," he said, "I want to talk to you. I want you to tell me about yourself so that I can remember it when I am here alone and try to pretend that you are still with me."

They sat side by side on the sofa in the Salon and Vania told him about her father and how adventurous he had always been and how he had made a huge fortune through his 'hunches', just as his father had done.

"My mother died when I was very young," she said, "and Papa took me about with him because he said it prevented him from being lonely."

"I can understand his feeling like that."

"Because he could not bear to live in the house where he had been so happy with Mama," Vania went on, "we rented houses in all sorts of strange places. For a year we lived in the North of Scotland, then Papa thought it would be amusing to go from there straight to Land's End.

"Because he could pay high rents and was prepared to take on other people's servants, their horses, everything that was necessary, the most magnificent mansions were put at our disposal. Castles, and once for six months, a Palace belonging to a member of the Royal Family."

"That must have intrigued you," Tyson smiled.

"I think all that it did," Vania answered, "was to make me long for a home of my own where I belonged and things belonged to me."

Tyson did not speak and she went on:

"That is why I love Revel Royal. It has been a home, and together we could make it . . . a place for love . . . a place for our . . . children."

She hardly breathed the words, but Tyson heard them.

"Vania!"

He rose from the sofa and went towards

176

the open window to stand looking out at the sky filled with stars, at the garden, a tangled mass of shadows.

"I am . . . sorry," Vania said.

"Come here!"

The words were a command and almost before he had spoken them Vania ran across the room to him.

He put his arm round her and drew her out onto the terrace. The stone balustrade was covered in lichen and moss and the ground was rough beneath their feet.

But Vania was only conscious that Tyson was touching her and when they reached the balustrade she looked up at him to see the outline of his face in the starlight.

"Tomorrow we have to leave each other through no fault of our own," Tyson said. "It is just that fate is us, but, my darling, because I know in my heart we belong to each other and because nobody else could ever mean what you mean to me, I am going to say goodbye to you now."

Vania did not reply, but she knew what he meant, and as she lifted her face to his, slowly, almost as if he was afraid he might frighten her, Tyson's lips came down on hers.

She felt his arms draw her against his heart, then as his mouth took possession of her, she knew that this was what she had been waiting for, this was what she had wanted from the first moment she had seen him.

He had been right when he said they belonged and she tried to draw herself closer and even closer to him until she became a part of him.

She could not explain her own feelings, she only felt as if something warm and wonderful moved up through her body into her breasts and again from her throat to her lips.

She felt as if she gave him her soul and he took it from her and made it his.

As Tyson felt her quiver against him, he knew that their kiss was an inexplicable magic that evoked within him an ecstasy that he had not even known existed but was part of life itself.

His kiss became more demanding, more insistent, and the rapture they both felt deepened until it embraced the whole world and touched the stars above them.

'This is love!' Vania thought to herself. 'This is love as I always knew it would be if only I could find it.'

She felt as if a shaft of starlight passed through her body and was so intense that it was a pain, and yet an ecstasy beyond words.

"I love you!" she wanted to cry.

She knew that Tyson loved her as she loved him and they were no longer two people but one.

He kissed her until the ground was no longer under her feet and she thought that they were both disembodied and floating above the earth into the sky.

Then at last as if human nature broke under the strain he raised his head to say:

"My darling! My precious! Could anyone be so perfect?"

His voice was unsteady.

For a moment Vania was speechless and she could only hide her face against him and know that if she was trembling, so was he.

"I love you!" Tyson said again. "I love you, and it is an agony that tears me in pieces. At the same time, it is a glory that makes me know I am the most fortunate man in the world."

"Oh, darling . . . darling!"

The words seemed to break from Vania's lips and she went on:

"I love you! Oh, Tyson, I love you! How can I . . . live without . . . you? How can I ever know . . . happiness again?"

She wanted to say so much more but his mouth came down on hers and she could only feel again that wild ecstasy for which there were no words.

When finally Vania found herself alone in her bedroom, she felt as if she was still floating in the clouds and it was impossible to think.

Then as she undressed slowly, she knew that the light of happiness had gone out and she was in a darkness which would envelop her for the rest of her life.

She wanted to go on kissing Tyson, to be in his arms, to know that he could evoke in her a wonder beyond anything she had ever dreamed or imagined was possible on this earth.

His kisses had brought her a spiritual ecstasy that she had thought was only known to those who died, and yet because she was still alive she would fall from the heights into the depths of despair.

She was still bemused and dazzled by the wonder of his kisses as he had drawn her back into the house and they had moved up the stairs together.

Only when she reached the door of her bedroom did she look at him with her heart in her eyes.

He had stood still seeming to take in the loveliness of her upturned face, the little movement of her hands reaching out towards him.

Then he said very quietly:

"Goodnight — goodbye — my little love! My only love!"

Almost before she could realise what had happened she was alone in her bedroom and the door was shut.

"It is . . . finished! Finished!" Vania said to herself.

Yet her mind could not comprehend it, and she could not really believe that he had 'thrown her out' as she had said once, jokingly, 'into the snow.'

She remembered how she had laughed and added:

"It would be easy to get back into this house through the broken windows or the doors which have no locks."

As she thought of it, she knew what she must do.

She would go to him and ask him if he would not marry her, then would he make her his mistress.

She was too innocent to know what this entailed, but she was aware that when two people married, they slept together and she thought that anything so intimate, so close, would be with Tyson even more wonderful than his kisses had been.

He had swept her up into a special Heaven and she thought that although she had reached the gates they had not been opened for her, yet that was what would happen if she belonged to him.

She knew that what she was suggesting would be thought wrong by other people, and yet she knew there was nothing wrong but everything that was right, perfect and sacred in her love for Tyson and his for her.

He would not tie her to him by marriage because he loved her too much for her to suffer in any way through such an arrangement.

But if she gave him herself and if they were one, as they were meant to be, man and woman complete because their love was greater than anything in the whole world, then at least she would have that to remember in the years to come.

Wearing only one of her thin attractive nightgowns Vania stood for a moment looking up at the stars through the open window.

"Please God, let him accept me," she prayed. "Let him make me his wife in love if not in name. I am his. You know I belong to him, and perhaps one day we can be together, as You meant us to be since we were born."

She almost expected that God would answer her and tell her to go to Tyson, but it flashed through her mind that perhaps He would think it wicked for them to love each other without the blessing of the Church.

Then she told herself that love was greater than anything else. Love was life, love was God. Love was the whole essence of living.

Resolutely, because she was afraid of her own courage she walked to the communicating door which connected their two bedrooms.

She turned the handle and pulled.

Then she knew that Tyson must have anticipated what she might do, for the door was locked!

Chapter 6

Vania came down the stairs as the grand-father clock in the Hall struck ten.

She was wearing the expensive blue travelling-gown in which she had arrived at Revel Royal and she knew, as she glanced in the mirror before she left her bedroom, that she looked very elegant and if she was honest, very lovely.

But her reflection merely made her feel more depressed than she was already.

What was the point of looking so different from what she felt?

An abject despair seemed to weigh down her whole body so that she felt as if she might sink into the ground itself.

Last night she had cried until she was exhausted, but even as she had done so, she knew that Tyson loved her and that alone saved her from wishing to die.

Wherever she might be in the future, he too would be somewhere in the world; and she could not help feeling that the fate that had introduced them to each other in such strange circumstances might, in the end, relent and allow them to be together, if only for a short time.

"I love . . . him! I love . . . him!" she had sobbed.

It was an inexpressible agony to know that just the other side of the locked door he was loving her too.

It seemed against everything that was natural and perfect that while she would wish to go to him because she loved him, he should lock her out because he loved her.

'We both want each other's happiness,' Vania thought, but knew the only thing that could make either of them really happy, was to be together.

She half-hoped when the dawn broke, that she could have breakfast with Tyson as she had done every morning since she had come to Revel Royal.

She tried to calculate if there would be time for them to have a last ride together and for her to change her clothes before the carriage, which was to carry her home, arrived from the village.

But when Mrs Briggs came to call her, she brought her breakfast on a tray.

This told Vania without words that Tyson

did not wish to see her until the moment came when she was to leave.

She wondered if he would change his mind and decide not to travel with her as he had promised, but send her alone, perhaps with Hawkins as an escort.

She tried to decide which would be the more agonising: to travel beside him knowing there was nothing more to say, or to drive away from Revel Royal leaving him behind.

When she was half-way down the stairs Tyson came from the Salon and stood waiting for her in the Hall.

She knew without even looking at him, that he was as tense and unhappy as she was.

The lines on his face seemed to be sharply etched and she knew his eyes would be dark with pain.

Because she loved him, she wanted to put her arms around him and comfort him, to tell him that things were not as bad as they seemed, that perhaps one day the barriers that separated them would vanish and they could love each other as they longed to do.

When she reached the Hall she moved towards Tyson while he stood still.

They looked at each other and he said in a voice that she found difficult to recognise because it was so low and hoarse:

"Are you — all right?"

"Yes . . . and you?"

There was no need for him to tell her how he was suffering and she knew that he saw the shadows under her eyes caused by her weeping and was aware that her lips were trembling.

"You have — packed your luggage?"

It was as if he forced himself to ask the commonplace because there was so much else he wanted to say.

"Yes . . . my trunks are . . . ready . . . they only need fastening down."

"I will do it."

Somehow, although she did not know why, she had an impulse to stop him from leaving her and going upstairs.

Even as she put out her hand towards him, he turned away and started to ascend the carved staircase, staring ahead of him, not looking down at her.

She watched him until he was out of sight, then like the trumpet of doom she heard the sound of carriage wheels and horses' hoofs outside the front door.

She thought she could not bear to look and turned her head to see old Briggs shuffling into the Hall from the passage which led to the kitchen.

"Is there anything I can get you, Miss Vania?" he asked.

"No . . . thank you," Vania replied.

As she spoke she saw Briggs look with surprise at the open doorway behind her and at the same time, she heard footsteps.

She supposed it was a groom from the Inn who had brought the carriage and that he had come into the house to help with the luggage.

She turned her head and was suddenly frozen into immobility.

It was not a stranger who stood there but Manfred Dale, looking flamboyantly impressive in a many-tiered riding-coat and with a high hat on his head.

She wanted to escape from him, to run away anywhere, but her feet seemed fastened to the ground and it was impossible even to breathe.

He took a step towards her and she opened her lips to scream.

As she did so, to her amazement, he produced a pistol from the pocket of his riding-coat.

"One sound to attract attention," he said, "and I will shoot this old fool down where he stands! I do not suppose you want that on your conscience?"

He pointed the pistol as he spoke, at

188

Briggs and Vania choked back the scream that was already in her throat.

"Come!" he said.

She had hardly realised what was happening when he seized her by the wrist and dragged her through the front door and down the steps.

Below her she saw a black and yellow Phaeton and recognised it as the one which Manfred Dale had been driving when he had visited her uncle's house.

But she had no time to see or think.

As they reached the Phaeton he picked her up in his arms and threw her onto the seat beside a man who was holding the reins.

As he did so the Phaeton began to move and Manfred Dale scrambled in beside her.

It all happened so quickly that only as the four horses swung away towards the bridge over the lake, did a thin scream escape from between Vania's lips.

"You can save your breath!" Manfred Dale said roughly. "No-one will hear you. If my bastard cousin intends to follow you he will find it impossible to catch up with us."

"How dare . . . you! How . . . dare you . . . treat me . . . like this!" Vania managed to gasp.

"If you behave in such a disreputable

manner with people with whom you have no right to associate," he retorted, "you must expect to receive what you deserve."

"Your cousin was taking me home today," Vania said defiantly, "so your high-handed action is quite unnecessary."

"If you had gone home I should merely have had the trouble of visiting you to make new arrangements for our marriage," Manfred Dale drawled. "I have therefore decided to take matters into my own hands."

"What do you mean by . . . that?" Vania asked suspiciously.

"I mean," he replied, "that I intend to marry you immediately!"

Vania stared at him in horror, then she said:

"Imme . . . diately?"

"Within an hour."

"I refuse! I absolutely refuse to marry you, now or at any time!" Vania cried.

"You are fortunate that I am willing to make an honest woman of you in spite of your staying alone and unchaperoned in that ramshackle house."

"Your cousin has behaved like a gentleman, which is more than you are doing, dragging me away by brute force, regardless of my feelings."

"I will make it up to you when you are my wife."

"That I have no intention of becoming," Vania retorted. "You may drag me to an altar, but I swear that you will not make me say the words that will make you legally my husband."

She drew in her breath and said:

"I hate you! Do you . . . understand? I hate you and . . . nothing in this world will make me . . . marry you!"

Manfred Dale laughed.

"You are a little spitfire!" he exclaimed. "It will amuse me to make you more compliant once you are my wife."

"You are not interested in me," Vania flashed, "but in my money. I overheard what you said to Tyson when you called at Revel Royal."

"So you were eavesdropping, were you?" Manfred Dale remarked. "I cannot believe you learnt anything you did not already know. After all, you could hardly have expected me to marry you, had you not been the possessor of a vast fortune."

"I loathe and despise you!" Vania cried. "You are everything that is low and despicable! It only astonishes me that any Society should accept you as one of its members!"

"You will find that there are a great many

191

benefits in being married to me."

"I suppose you are referring to the fact that your father has unfairly assumed a title which is not lawfully his."

"That is where you are wrong," Manfred Dale said. "It *is* lawfully his. My Uncle Hubert conveniently forgot to marry the woman of his fancy, and that is certainly something that will not happen in your case."

"I have . . . told you I will not . . . marry you."

"I can assure you that you have no choice."

There was something so positive and confident in Manfred Dale's voice that Vania felt herself shiver.

She wondered how he could force her into saying 'I will' in front of a Parson, and she felt fear flicker inside her like something evil and menacing.

She also became uncomfortably aware that because she was squeezed between the driver of the Phaeton and Manfred Dale, they were very close together.

His arm rested on the turned back hood behind her, and although she tried to move further away from him, her knees were against his.

He was a large man and she felt very small and insignificant beside him. She knew too that he could overpower her easily and it would be hopeless to try to struggle or escape from him.

They had passed through the village and now they were on a main road which Vania suspected led towards London.

She tried to see a milestone to determine where they were going but the horses were moving too quickly and she thought despairingly that every moment she was being carried further and further away from Tyson.

Because she was afraid, her first bewilderment at being dragged from the house and into the Phaeton had made it hard for her to think clearly.

But she now began to consider more calmly what she should say, what she should do to extricate herself from this appalling position.

They drove on for a little way before she said in a conciliatory tone:

"Please . . . Mr Dale . . . take me home to my uncle . . . I realise we are driving towards London . . . but once I am home we can discuss this quietly . . . and that I am certain . . . would be easier for both of us."

"It will not be easier for me," Manfred Dale replied. "I have decided to marry you without all the frills and furbelows of a grand wedding, and once you are my wife I will think of a good explanation if anyone should ask questions."

"I have already . . . told you that I will not marry you . . . and certainly not with this . . . unseemly haste."

"How am I to know it is not necessary?"

"What do you . . . mean by that?"

"I mean you have been staying alone with my unpredictable cousin. Surely he was man enough to take advantage of the fact?"

It was impossible not to understand the sneer and the innuendo not only in Manfred Dale's words, but in his voice and Vania gave a little cry of sheer horror.

"How can you . . . suggest such a . . . thing? Your cousin is . . . everything that is fine and decent . . . different in . . . every possible way from . . . you!"

"If you talk to me like that," Manfred Dale warned sharply, "I shall give you a good shaking. All my life I have had Tyson held up to me as an example of everything I ought to be, and I am not going to stand it from the woman who bears my name, you may be certain of that!"

He spoke so sharply, forgetting to drawl, that Vania knew she had touched him on the raw.

This, she thought to herself, was one of the reasons why he was so cock-a-hoop at his father being able to assume the title which was by right Tyson's.

Because she wished to press home the advantage she had found unexpectedly, she said:

"I can assure you of one thing, your Cousin Tyson would never force any woman to do anything against her will."

"My Cousin Tyson should have had nothing to do with you," Manfred Dale replied sulkily. "I realise now he only came across you by chance when, again by chance, you were obliged to stay the night at the *Dog and Duck*."

"How did you learn that?" Vania asked.

"I have put together the whole story," Manfred Dale replied, "and I know without your telling me what happened. That swine Blakely tried to abduct you, Tyson saved you from him and thought while he was about it, he might as well pick up an heiress for himself."

"That is the one thing he did not think," Vania retorted. "I begged him . . . pleaded with him, to take me away, simply because I have no . . . wish to . . . marry you."

Manfred Dale laughed.

"A reluctant kidnapper? I am sure my sanctimonious cousin had it on the list of sins he should not commit. It is at least, re-

assuring to know that I shall not be fa-
thering another bastard, even if it would be
one of the family!"

"How . . . dare you . . . speak to me like . . .
that?" Vania said in a low voice.

She clenched her fingers together at the
insult, and she knew that if she had a dagger
in her hand, she would strike him with it.

She had never in her life, felt such a wave
of hatred and contempt as she felt for this
man beside her with his sneering remarks,
his way of making everything seem dirty and
coarse.

It suddenly struck her that apart from
anything else every word of their conversation must have been overheard by the
groom who was driving.

She wondered how any man who called
himself a gentleman could say such outrageous things in front of a servant.

"Well, one thing is very obvious,"
Manfred Dale said after a moment, as if he
had been thinking over what she had said,
"we can start our married life, my dear
Evangeline, without any pretence. Once I
have the handling of your money, you can
do what you like for all I care, and if you
wish to return to the uncomfortable hovel
from which I have just rescued you, I shall
not put any obstacles in your way."

Vania felt words of contempt rise to her lips, when a sudden thought struck her.

"Supposing," she suggested slowly, "I offer you my . . . fortune without . . . me? Would not that . . . solve both our . . . problems?"

Manfred Dale obviously considered the proposition for a moment, then he said:

"I have not seen your father's will, but I am quite certain it would be legally impossible for your Guardian to hand over the money you possess to anyone other than your husband."

Vania felt the little hope that had been lit in her heart flicker out.

She was intelligent enough to know that Manfred Dale was speaking the truth.

Her uncle with her father's Solicitor were the Guardians of her enormous fortune until she married, then by law everything she possessed became the property of her husband.

It would certainly be illegal for them to give Manfred Dale, or any other person, her money unless she was his wife.

She looked ahead, seeing the horses devour the road in front of them, while the speed at which they were travelling was throwing out great clouds of dust behind them.

There was silence for at least a mile. Then

Manfred Dale spoke over her head to the groom who was driving.

"The next village, Bill. You will see the Church on the left."

"The . . . Church?"

As Vania asked the question she turned her face swiftly towards his.

"It is where we are to be married."

"But . . . you cannot . . . I will not . . . I refuse!"

The words seemed to tumble from Vania's lips.

"I have already made the arrangements," Manfred Dale replied, "and the Parson will be waiting for us."

"I have . . . told you," Vania said, "that I will not . . . marry you."

As she spoke she saw with a feeling of horror, that just ahead of them through the trees there was a grey spire of the Church.

Desperately she tried to think what she could do.

Surely whatever Manfred Dale might say, no Parson would marry her if she told him she was being coerced into marriage against her will?

'I am under age, my Guardian is not here. He must listen to me!' she told herself desperately.

They were drawing nearer and nearer to

the Church and now she could see it set back a little way from the road with the churchyard in front of it.

There was a lychgate opening onto a flagged path which led to a porch jutting out from the grey stone building.

"I will not marry you!" she said aloud in a tone of resolute defiance.

Manfred Dale smiled a twisted smile that she thought when she had first met him, had something evil about it.

"In which case I shall shoot the Parson in a manner which will doubtless cripple him for the rest of his life!"

Vania made an inaudible murmur of horror and he went on, drawling the words slowly:

"I will not kill him, mind you, which would lead to unpleasant repercussions, just maim him. Then we will travel onto the next Church and the next until there is a whole string of suffering, bleeding Parsons left behind us. Is that what you want? It would certainly be a quite original way to get married!"

"You are a fiend . . . a devil," Vania cried. "How can you think of anything so cruel and horrible?"

"It is up to you," Manfred Dale replied. "Marry me quietly and there will be no casualties to mar the happiness of your wedding-day!"

Vania stared at him in horror as the Phaeton came to a standstill outside the lychgate.

Manfred Dale stepped down, then as Vania had not moved, held out his hand.

"Come along, my charming bride," he said sarcastically. "I know how much you are longing, as I am, for us to be man and wife — one flesh, as the Church puts it."

He was taunting her, Vania knew, but all she could do was wonder desperately how she could escape, if there was a way out of this hideous situation.

She wanted to think that he was bluffing, that he would not if she refused to marry him, really shoot the Parson as he had threatened. Yet she had the uncomfortable feeling that to possess her fortune Manfred Dale would stick at nothing.

"Oh, Papa," Vania cried in her heart, "why did you leave me any money? Why am I to be the prey of a man like this?"

"Come along," Manfred Dale said impatiently.

Vania knew that if she refused he would drag her forcibly from the Phaeton regardless of how undignified she might appear in the process.

Because there was nothing she could do but obey, because every avenue of escape seemed closed, she slowly, with a reluctance that was not only physical but mental, allowed him to help her from the Phaeton to the ground.

She glanced towards the small village which lay beyond the Church and wondered if there could be any help there.

Then she knew if she tried to run away Manfred Dale would forcibly prevent her from doing so, and if she screamed would doubtless put his hand over her mouth.

She felt as if she could not bear to be touched by him, as if every nerve in her body shrank away from him, and even as she was wondering what she could do, she felt her feet carrying her automatically along the path that led to the door of the Church.

She stopped and looking up at Manfred Dale, said in a whisper:

"Please . . . please . . . do not do this . . . not now . . . not at this moment . . . we must talk about it . . . I will try to . . . agree to what you want . . . but do not make me . . . marry you . . . now."

"You have escaped me once," Manfred Dale replied. "I do not intend that you shall do so again!"

There was a determination in his voice

which told her that to plead any further however much she humiliated herself, would be of no avail.

"Oh, God," she prayed in her heart, "help me . . . help me!"

Then as they walked into the Church she found herself calling desperately to the man she loved.

"Tyson! Tyson!"

Her whole being seemed to echo his name over and over again as if it was a talisman.

But even as her very spirit went out to him, she saw a Clergyman wearing a surplice walk into the Chancel to stand at the altar-steps waiting for them . . .

Tyson, carrying one of Vania's smaller trunks, came to the top of the stairs.

He put it down and seeing Briggs standing below, called:

"Where is Hawkins? I want him to give me a hand with the luggage."

"Oh, Master Tyson! Master Tyson!" Briggs cried in a frightened voice. "I've never known anything like it in all me born days. He threatened to shoot me, Master Tyson!"

"What are you talking about?" Tyson asked.

"Mr Manfred, Sir! He dragged Miss

Vania down the steps. If I hadn't seen it with me own eyes I'd never have believed it, that I wouldn't!"

"What on earth are you saying?" Tyson demanded. "What has happened?"

He came hurrying down the stairs and as he did so Hawkins came in through the front door.

"It's true, Sir," he said. "The gentleman as called the other day in the yellow and black Phaeton pulled Miss Vania down the steps. Then he picks her up, flings her into the Phaeton and jumps in beside her!"

"He says," chimed in Briggs, " 'If you make a sound I'll shoot that old fool!' "

Tyson picked up his hat and whip which was lying on the table in the Hall.

"Is Salamanca outside?"

"Yes, Sir. And Vittoria. I brought them round as you told me to."

Tyson did not answer. He merely ran down the steps to fling himself onto Salamanca's back.

He moved off at such a pace that Hawkins, who was slower in mounting Vittoria, only caught up with him when he was half-way down the drive.

It was fortunate, Tyson thought, if anything could be thought fortunate at this moment, that he had decided that he and

Hawkins should act as out-riders to the carriage which was to carry Vania home.

He knew it would be impossible for him to sit beside her and not take her in his arms and kiss her as he had done last night.

When finally they had parted and gone upstairs to bed he had known that both of them had reached breaking-point.

If he had loved Vania before when he kissed her, he had known that saying they belonged to each other and were a part of each other, were not idle words.

She was completely and absolutely his, and it was only years of self-control that had prevented him from telling her that however wrong it might be from her point of view, they would be married.

He had known it was what Vania wanted him to say. He had known too that she gave him her heart and soul in her kiss and was ready to give him anything else he might ask of her.

But he had forced himself to remember how young she was, how little she had seen of the world, and how because he loved her as a man he must protect her from everything that would hurt, harm or spoil her, and that included himself.

When he had gone to his room, his whole being throbbed with an unbearable agony because she was so near. Yet he placed her as far away from him in his mind, as if he had imprisoned her on the moon.

He had locked the communicating-door between their rooms not, as Vania thought, to lock her out but since it had never crossed his mind for one moment that she would come to him, to prevent himself from forgetting everything, even his honour, and making her his because his whole being needed her in a manner that swept away reason, commonsense and wisdom.

"I want her! God, I want her!" Tyson had said looking up at the stars under which he had kissed her.

Because he knew he would not sleep, he had stood at his window for half the night, looking out on the romantic beauty of the moonlight on the lake and the mystery of the sleeping garden.

What he saw, however, was Vania's face and the long empty years ahead when he would be without her.

It seemed to him almost impossible that he could have fallen in love so completely and hopelessly within a few days of leaving the Army and his previous life behind.

For thirteen years he had been a soldier, eight of them beside men who now were scattered all over the country and whom he might never see again.

For these last years he had had only one object in his mind — to win the war and to see that as many as possible of those who had served with him, should stay alive.

There had been moments of privation, hunger and fear. There had also been times of comradeship, of laughter and of triumph.

He had wondered when he reached Dover what he would find in England that was hard to remember. He was well aware that many changes had taken place.

What he had certainly not expected was that he would fall in love and be beset by emotions and sensations that were different from anything he had felt or known before.

It was not only because Vania was very lovely and he had been deprived of the company of women for a long time, it was because he knew there was some magnetism between them that was inescapable.

She might be younger than he was by several years, her education might have been different, she might be rich while he was poor.

But none of that mattered beside the fact that they belonged, perhaps in a dozen previous lives, and their souls had recognised each other from the moment they met.

"She is mine," Tyson said to himself,

"mine absolutely and completely. I love her, I adore her, I worship her. Not for the first time, but all through the ages."

It struck him that, in this case, they would never be able to escape each other and they would meet again.

But that was a philosophy for thinkers and scholars.

A very human part of him wanted Vania now. He wanted to kiss her, to make her his, and for them to live together and create children that were a part of their love.

"Vania! Oh Vania!"

It seemed to him that the world sang with the music of her name, and the beauty of the Universe was in her face and the stars in her eyes.

Only when he was tired out and exhausted mentally did Tyson move from the window to throw himself down on the great bed despairingly, feeling there was only a few hours before Vania would leave his house and his life.

Nothing could ever be the same again.

Now riding in hot pursuit of the yellow and black Phaeton which carried her away from him, Tyson knew his anger against Manfred was so uncontrollable that when he caught up with them it would be hard not to murder his cousin.

As boys they had always hated each other and he had heard many stories of Manfred's behaviour at school which had made him ashamed of their relationship.

Manfred was a bully and the smaller boys were terrified of him. He was also rude to the servants and completely insensitive to the demands of any service he required of them.

Tyson had always thought the less he saw of his cousin the better, for although there was a family feud he had, for his mother's sake, deprecated it.

His father had always said the less he saw of his brother George the better, but Tyson was sensitive enough to realise that his mother felt that it was her fault that the brothers were estranged.

Actually George Dale, like his son, had such an unpleasant character that it was doubtful, Tyson thought, if his father would have had much to do with them, whoever he had married.

Yet because his mother blamed herself for the break between them, he was determined he would never personally make things worse.

But now, he told himself with fury, Manfred would, when he caught up with him, suffer for his outrageous behaviour towards Vania.

They had ridden for nearly an hour and Tyson had pushed Salamanca to such a speed that it was hard for Vittoria to keep up.

"Do you think Miss Vania's been taken to London?" Hawkins shouted above the clatter of the horses' hooves.

"I think so," Tyson replied, "although I have no particular reason for being sure of it."

He thought to himself that Manfred would take Vania to his parents, and then insist that they be married as quickly as possible.

He suspected that his cousin would not risk her being abducted or spirited away from him for the second time, which might easily happen in her own home.

Vania would therefore, from his point of view, be safer at Wellingdale House in Park Lane, than anywhere else.

It came back to Tyson very forcefully how much had been appropriated which should, in fact, have been his.

There was not only Wellingdale House in Hertfordshire, one of the finest examples of Queen Anne architecture in the whole country.

There was also the London house, a Hunting Lodge in Leicestershire, and a place in Scotland where his Grandfather had found the game-shooting and salmon fishing particularly agreeable.

It seemed incredible that so much that should have been his had been stolen while he was away, without his even having a chance to protest at such piracy.

Yet he told himself frankly, if he had been there, what could he have said that old Chessington had not said for him.

Perhaps Vania was right, they would find the proof of his father's and mother's marriage hidden away in some secret place at Revel Royal. But until he did so, Tyson knew that he had no case to take to the Courts.

He rode on, still moving at a pace which made Hawkins wonder how long Vittoria could keep it up.

He knew Salamanca was an exceedingly strong horse and had a stamina that had been remarkable in the battlefield.

Hawkins thought it was unlikely that there was a horse in the whole of England who could have gone faster than they were travelling at this moment, and he knew, if only they were on the right road, they would sooner or later catch up the team of horses which belonged to Manfred Dale.

It had been a stroke of good fortune that the horses were at the door when their Master had wanted them.

It would have taken at least five minutes, Hawkins calculated, to run to the stables and saddle Salamanca and Vittoria. Five minutes that might be precious, perhaps even vital.

He did not know why he thought that, but it just came to his mind.

As it did so, he gave a sudden gasp.

"Look, Sir! Look!" he shouted.

He pointed as he spoke and Tyson looking ahead, saw what had excited Hawkins' attention.

There was a yellow and black Phaeton pulled up outside the stone wall of a village Churchyard.

Tyson did not even slacken his pace.

"The groom holding the reins is yours, Hawkins," he cried.

He increased Salamanca's speed as he spoke, and waited to pull the stallion up abruptly on his haunches directly behind the Phaeton.

As he flung himself from the saddle, Tyson realised that Hawkins had sprung from Vittoria straight onto the groom in the Phaeton, but he did not wait to see what happened.

He ran down the path and as he pushed open the Church door he heard a voice say:

"Will you, Manfred, take this . . ."

"Stop this marriage!" Tyson cried.

His voice seemed to ring out and echo round the small Church.

Then as he stepped forward Vania turned and gave a little scream.

"Be careful," she cried. "He has a . . . pistol!"

Even as her voice seemed to echo as Tyson's had done, Manfred drew the pistol from the pocket of his coat.

As he did so, the Parson standing on the step above the couple in front of him, shut his prayer-book and slapped it hard against Manfred Dale's face.

It only made him stagger but in that split moment of time Tyson reached him.

He thrust up his cousin's arm and there was a resounding explosion.

As the bullet struck a pillar, Tyson hit Manfred with all his force on the chin.

He staggered but before he could fall, Tyson followed it with a smashing blow to the nose.

He felt the bone crack beneath his knuckles. Manfred collapsed, falling backwards on the flagged floor and was still.

As Tyson looked down at him to be certain he was unconscious he heard Vania give a cry.

Then she flung herself against him.

"You . . . came! You . . . came. I prayed you . . . would save me."

Tyson held her so tightly that she could barely breathe.

"It is all right, my darling."

He looked over her head towards the Parson.

"Thank you . . ." he began, then exclaimed, "Good Heavens, it is you, Padre!"

The Parson smiled.

"I see you are in your usual form, Major. An exceptional right and left."

"Thank you, Padre, but it was your preliminary manoeuvre that gave me the opportunity to get at him."

Vania raised her head from Tyson's shoulder looking a little bewildered.

"This is the Reverend Augustus Henderson, darling," he explained. "He was the Chaplain of my Regiment."

"I am staying here with my brother until I can find a living of my own," the Reverend Henderson explained. "I felt there was something wrong about this marriage."

He glanced at the man lying on the ground before he said:

"But he had a Special Licence signed by

the Archbishop of Canterbury, and there was nothing I could do about it."

"A Special Licence?" Tyson asked sharply. "Where is it?"

"In the Vestry," the Chaplain replied.

"Wait here, my precious," Tyson said to Vania.

He walked from the Chancel through a door which he could see would lead him into the Vestry and the Chaplain and Vania stood looking after him in surprise.

He was away only for a few seconds, but when he returned he was holding the Special Licence in his hand.

"I have altered a few words, Padre," he said, and held up the Licence so that both he and Vania could read it.

On it had been written 'Manfred Dale, son of Lord Wellingdale'. Tyson had changed the Christian name to 'Tyson' and inserted the word 'grand' before 'son'.

There was silence for a moment. Then he said quietly:

"I think, Padre, in the circumstances this is legal enough to enable you to marry me to someone I love very deeply, and who I know loves me."

"There is nothing that would give me greater pleasure, Major," the Chaplain answered.

Vania gave a little cry and it seemed to hold all the happiness in the world in one sound.

"Do you . . . mean it? Do you . . . really mean it?" she whispered to Tyson. "It is what I have . . . prayed for."

"I have to take care of you," he said. "Everything else seems unimportant."

"It is!" she answered.

She slipped her hand into Tyson's and as if there was no longer any need for words, they stood in front of the Chaplain with their faces raised to his.

He smiled at them before he opened his book and again began the Marriage Service.

As they came out of the Church it seemed to Vania that the sun was more golden than it had ever been and the birds were singing with angel voices that were echoed by the music in her heart.

She was holding tightly on to Tyson's hand as the Chaplain walked beside them down the flagged path towards the lychgate.

Then as they reached it, they saw that Hawkins was sitting in the driver's seat of the Phaeton keeping the team under control, while Salamanca and Vittoria were quite unconcernedly cropping the grass beside the road.

They all looked at Hawkins, then saw there was a crumpled body over the Churchyard wall sprawling on top of a grave.

They walked to the Phaeton. Hawkins' knuckles were bleeding and one eye was swollen and half-closed, but he was grinning triumphantly.

"Well done, Hawkins!" Tyson said.

Then just as he was about to reply, Hawkins saw the Chaplain.

"Bless me, if it ain't the Padre!" he exclaimed.

"Yes, Hawkins," the Chaplain replied, "and I have told you before about lowering your guard."

"He was a bit more spry than I anticipated, Sir," Hawkins replied, "but I hammered him in the end."

"So I see," the Chaplain smiled.

"I must explain, darling," Tyson said to Vania, "that the Padre was a very efficient boxing instructor when there was no-one else available."

"I am not going to comment on how good a pugilist your husband was," the Chaplain remarked. "You have seen him in action yourself."

"I believe he is good at everything!" Vania answered.

Tyson's fingers tightened on hers, and he said:

"I think the best way I can get you home is to drive you in the Phaeton, and Hawkins can manage the two horses."

There was laughter in his voice as he said to the Chaplain:

"When my cousin is capable of understanding what you say to him, would you be obliging enough to inform him that his Phaeton and horses will be stabled at his expense at the *Dog and Duck* at Little Fenwick?"

"I will give him your message."

The Chaplain held out his hand and Tyson said:

"Give us a little time to enjoy our honeymoon, Padre, then come and visit us at Revel Royal. Your brother will tell you where it is."

"I accept your invitation with the greatest of pleasure," the Chaplain answered.

Tyson took over the reins from Hawkins and with Vania beside him they drove away.

The moment they were out of sight of the Church, Vania moved a little closer to him and in a voice that seemed to hold the sunshine in it:

"We are married . . . we are really married! I am your . . . wife and you are my . . . husband!"

"And I hope it is something you will never regret," Tyson said quietly.

"Do you imagine that is . . . likely? Oh, darling, darling Tyson, I called to you, and when you came into the Church I knew God had sent you to . . . save me."

"There may be a lot of difficulties ahead," Tyson said gravely, "and I cannot believe that your uncle will be very pleased at what has happened. But somehow we shall have to convince him that there is nothing he can do."

"Do you . . . think he will . . . try to . . . separate us?" Vania asked.

"I think from the state in which we have left my cousin," Tyson said dryly, "it will be some time before he is well enough to communicate with your uncle, and in the circumstances he may think it wiser not to create a scandal."

"I do not think I could . . . bear to lose you . . . again," Vania said. "I was so unhappy last night . . . so utterly and completely miserable that I could not imagine how I could go on living without you . . . but now . . ."

She turned her face up to Tyson.

"I love you! Oh, Tyson, I love you in a

way that is . . . impossible to put into . . . words."

"There will be no need for words when we get home, my darling," Tyson replied.

Chapter 7

Vania and Tyson walked along the corridor from the Dining-Room.

He had his arm around her and she felt as if they floated on clouds of happiness.

"I have never had a more delicious and wonderful meal!" she exclaimed.

"That is what I felt, my darling," Tyson answered.

She gave a little laugh and asked:

"What did we eat?"

He laughed too.

"I have not the slightest idea! I only know because I was looking at you, that I have never enjoyed anything more."

"What am I wearing?"

"I have only seen your face."

"Do you . . . like it?"

"I find it irresistible."

"I hoped you would . . . admire my gown!"

"I admire and want to see more of what is inside it."

"Tyson!"

"Have I shocked you, my lovely one?"

"N–no . . . I am not . . . shocked," Vania replied, "only . . . shy."

"I adore you when you are shy."

"It is a . . . different shyness," she whispered, "with little thrills running up and down . . . my spine."

"My precious!"

Tyson kissed her forehead as they walked into the Salon. The candles were not lit and the light came from the sky outside.

He looked down at Vania and drew her close against his heart.

"You are right," he said. "The whole house is enchanted. Never has this room looked so attractive and never, my darling, and this is the truth, has it held anybody so beautiful or so perfect."

His arms tightened as he spoke, and he paused for a moment as he looked at her face, as if he could hardly believe what he saw.

Then his lips sought hers and he kissed her with a slow, demanding kiss which, as he felt her respond, grew more passionate.

She moved closer and still closer, wanting to be part of him, feeling as if the whole world was radiant with a wonder which came from within themselves, and yet was part of the house and the glory of the setting sun outside . . .

"I love you! Oh, Tyson . . . I love . . . you," she whispered.

Later Tyson drew Vania through the open window and onto the terrace.

"This is where I kissed you goodbye, my precious," he said, "and I meant honestly to let you go, because I thought it would be for your happiness."

"It would . . . never have been . . . that," Vania murmured.

"Fate decided otherwise," he went on. "I knew when I was just in time to stop you from marrying my despicable cousin that you belonged to me and it would be wicked to let anything so trivial as money or even my good name stand in the way of our love."

Vania gave a little murmur of happiness and put her head against his shoulder.

"I knew that," she said. "I always knew it. Nothing, and I mean nothing, my wonderful Tyson, is important besides the fact that we love each other."

He kissed her hair as she went on:

"Last night I was so happy that I wanted to . . . die. Now all I want to do is to live with you and love you for the rest of our lives."

"That is what we will do, my sweet,"

Tyson said, "but God knows what sort of life it is going to be."

"It will be wonderful, magical, ecstatic, because we are together."

"I hope you will say that again in five — ten — fifteen years' time," he replied. "When I look at you and know you are the most beautiful person I have ever seen, I am afraid."

"Why?"

"Because I shall never be able to buy you all the things I want to give you."

He looked across the garden to where the sun was setting behind the ancient oak-trees in the Park.

"If I could dress you in the rainbow," he said in a low voice, "and give you a necklace of stars, that would be only a tiny part of what your beauty deserves."

"I would . . . rather have your . . . kisses."

Vania lifted her lips to his and saw the fire in his eyes as his mouth came down on hers.

The candle was burning low behind the curtain but it still suffused the room with a soft golden light, enough for Tyson to see Vania's eyes and her fair hair streaming over his shoulder.

"Do you still love me, my darling?" he asked.

"Love you? I adore you! Oh Tyson, how could you ever have made me . . . leave you when you . . . knew we could feel like . . . this?"

"Like what?" he questioned with a smile.

"How can I put it into words?" Vania asked. "I feel as if I was no longer myself, but part of the sunshine and the flowers . . . part too of the moonlight, the stars and . . . you."

There was a passionate note in her voice that was very moving and Tyson said:

"That is how I want to make you feel, my perfect little wife."

"There are no . . . words to describe what it is like to . . . fly into the heart of the sun," Vania whispered, "or dive down into the . . . depth of the . . . ocean. Oh Tyson, Tyson, why did nobody tell me that love was so . . . wonderful?"

He held her a little closer and she went on:

"If I had known I swear . . . nothing would have made me . . . leave you, and if you had . . . turned me out I would have sat on the . . . doorstep until you took me in again."

"Now you are mine, my darling," Tyson said in a deep voice, "you will never sit on the doorstep but be against my heart so that I can protect you, look after you, and I swear that if I can prevent it, you shall never be unhappy again."

Vania put up her arms to draw his head down to hers and this time she kissed him at first very gently on the lips.

Then as he felt a little quiver go through her, their lips clung to each other.

"I love . . . you! I love . . . you!" she cried.

But she was not certain whether she spoke the words aloud.

All she knew was that once again Tyson was carrying her into the heart of the sun and she felt her whole body burning with the wonder of it.

The candle had guttered lower still but there was enough light to illuminate two heads on one pillow.

"You must go to sleep, my precious," Tyson said. "You have had a long day and there is a lot to do tomorrow, when we must go on with our search for what you call 'my treasure'."

"I know it is . . . here somewhere in this . . . house," Vania said drowsily, "but now there is no . . . hurry, and I no longer have that . . . desperate feeling that the sands are . . . running out and you will send me . . . away before we have . . . found your fortune."

"It will be hard to look anywhere except

into your eyes, but as you say, my precious, there is no longer any hurry."

He moved his lips across her forehead before he added:

"I too was utterly miserable and unhappy last night. How could I have guessed that twenty-four hours would change everything and you would belong to me?"

"I am . . . all yours," Vania murmured, "and I thought when we were being married, how pleased Papa would have been that we had been adventurous as he always was, and that you had followed what was undoubtedly a 'hunch' that I should be your wife."

"It was more than that," Tyson said. "It was an irresistible desire that I could no longer control."

"I am . . . glad . . . so very . . . glad."

She paused, then she said a little shyly:

"I think your . . . mother would be . . . glad too that we are here . . . together in her room."

"I am sure she would be," Tyson said, "and she would have loved you."

"I never told you that I dreamt of your mother the other night."

"What did you dream?" he asked.

"I was going to tell you about it when I came downstairs," Vania said. "In fact I began when old Briggs remembered the silver, and we found 'Treasure Number Two'."

"I remember now!" Tyson exclaimed. "You said: 'I had an extraordinary dream last night'. Tell me about it now."

"I dreamt that your mother was sitting in this room," Vania replied. "I could see her very clearly, and I was sure it was your mother because she looked a little like you and her hair was the same colour."

"That is right," Tyson smiled.

"She had a very sweet, spiritual face and she was sitting writing with a very big quill pen in a very small book."

Tyson did not speak and Vania went on:

"I suppose it was because we had been looking at books all the evening in the Library but in my dream I remember thinking how small the book was in comparison with the pen."

She felt Tyson stiffen.

"What is it?" she asked.

"A very small book!" Tyson repeated in a strange voice.

"That is what I saw in my dream."

"A diary!" he exclaimed in a voice that seemed unnaturally loud. "My mother always kept a diary. I never thought of it until this moment!"

"Oh, Tyson . . . do you think . . . ?"

"Where can she have kept them? Have you seen any diaries here in this room?" Tyson asked.

"The book was very small," Vania answered, "and perhaps that is where it is . . . over there."

She pointed as she spoke and Tyson looked across the room to where, on either side of the fireplace, there were two cases with shell-like tops set into the wall.

The three bottom shelves in each of the cases were filled with small, leather-bound books and on the shelves above were tiny attractive pieces of china, little Dresden cupids, Rockingham lambs and other small animals.

Tyson began to get out of bed and Vania cried:

"I noticed them, but I thought they were books of poetry. I meant to examine them sometime . . . but there have been so . . . many other . . . things to do."

Tyson picked up his robe which lay over a chair and put it on, then lighting a new candle from the one which was almost extinguished, he carried it across the room and set it down on the marble mantelshelf.

He stood for a moment looking at the rows of leather-bound books and Vania watching him, prayed they would be his mother's diaries and contain the information he needed so desperately.

Then almost as if he was afraid, Tyson put out his hand tentatively and drew out the first small book.

He opened it while Vania held her breath.

"These *are* my mother's diaries," he said in a voice that did not sound like his own, "and this one is dated 1776 when my mother was fifteen."

He replaced it and moved along the row.

He drew out another book and turned the leaves very carefully, moving a little nearer to the lighted candies as he did so.

"In what year did your father and mother run away together?" Vania asked, feeling she could hardly bear the tension.

"In 1782," Tyson answered, "and I am almost sure that it was in the summer."

As he finished speaking he turned another page and gave an exclamation. It was a sound that made Vania say quickly:

"Read it to me, Tyson. I must . . . know what you have . . . found."

Tyson walked back to the bedside and sat down on the mattress, and Vania hastily pulled back the curtain so that the light was enough for him to read by.

"Listen to this," he said.

Vania could see that the writing in the little book was very neat and at the same time had an elegance which she had always connected in her mind with Tyson's mother.

"The page is headed *Calais, June 16th,*" Tyson said and read aloud:

"We arrived here Two days ago but this is the First Chance I have had to Write down all the Thrilling and Exciting things that have Happened to Me.

"On Tuesday morning I woke up very early and crept out of the House while Papa and Mama were still Asleep. I had packed my leather bag the night before, and even though I put very few Things in it because Dearest Hubert said he would buy me Everything I wanted when we reached France, it was still Heavy.

"But I managed to Carry it through the' Garden to where Hubert was Waiting for me amongst the Lilac bushes, just out of Sight of the House.

"He took me in His arms and Kissed me, and I knew then that Nothing mattered except that We should be Together, even though I knew Papa

would be very Angry when he found out I had Gone.

"We hurried through the Shrubbery and waiting on the Road there was a Post Chaise drawn by four Horses. Once We started off Hubert took me in his Arms and I was no longer Afraid, and not for one Moment did I regret that I had done anything so Reprehensible as to Run away with Him.

"The miles to Dover seemed to Speed past and only when we Reached the Town did I ask Hubert where we were to be Married but he told me with a smile that it was a Secret. Of course I was completely Happy to leave Everything in His capable Hands but I was Surprised when We did not stop until the Horses drew up at the Quayside.

"We got out and Hubert had our Luggage carried to a Boat and a man rowed us out into the Harbour. Then I saw where we were going. There was a magnificent Frigate anchored ahead of us. I could read the name H.M.S. Formidable.

"It was very Exciting to climb Aboard even though I found the Rope-ladder rather Difficult, but there were plenty of *willing Hands to help Me. When we were on Deck Hubert introduced Me to the Captain, a gentleman called Edward Dawson, who was a very old Friend of His.*

"We went down Below into what I found was a surprisingly large and comfortable Cabin, and Captain Dawson said to Hubert:

" 'I think the sooner the Ceremony takes place the Better because it may be a bit Choppy once we get to Sea.'

"I looked at Hubert in Surprise and He said:

" 'It is perfectly Right and Legal, my Dearest, for the Captain of a ship to Marry any of his Passengers, and I thought This would be not only an Original manner for Us to be Wed, but also a way that We can keep it Secret until You come of Age.'

"He then looked at the Captain and asked:

" 'Is that not right, Edward?'

" 'Your Marriage, Ma'am,' the Captain said to me, 'will be Entered in the Ship's Log, and You will sign your Names under my Signature which makes Your Marriage completely legal. It will take Me at least a Year,

*perhaps Longer, to complete the Log
and only then will it go to the Admiralty
to be Filed with the Logs of all the other
Ships of His Majesty's Fleet.'*

"When he said that he smiled at
Hubert and said:

" 'Even then it is extremely Doubtful
if Anyone will read it. If You ask me
Your Secret will be Safe for a great
number of Years, if not for Ever!'

" 'That is all We want,' Hubert said
taking my Hand. The Captain had His
Prayer-Book ready, and We were
Married!"*

Tyson ceased reading and looked at
Vania but for the moment she thought that
he did not see her. Instead there was an expression of triumph and relief on his face.

" *We were married!'* " he repeated beneath his breath. "That is all I wanted to find
out! That is what I knew had happened!"

"Oh, Tyson, I am so glad!" Vania cried.

"Now my mother's name will be cleared,"
he said, "and my uncle will apologise in
abject humility for ever having cast asper-
sions on her."

He closed the diary and for a moment laid
his hand on it almost reverently.

"We will read the rest of this tomorrow,

my precious," he said. "We have found everything that matters."

"Oh, Tyson, I am so glad . . . so very, very . . . glad!"

"So am I!"

He stood up but as Vania knew he was going to take off his robe and get back into bed, she gave a sudden cry.

"What is it?" he asked.

"Have you not thought that if your mother wrote about her marriage, she would also have written later of anything so important as your father hiding his fortune here in the house?"

Tyson's hands which were undoing the cord at the waist of his robe were still.

"Of course!" he exclaimed. "She would certainly have recorded that."

"In which year did it happen?" Vania enquired.

"My father died at the end of 1809 and Chessington told me it was early in the year that he had his 'hunch' that the Bank was going to close."

"Then look at that date quickly!" Vania replied. "It will be on the other side of the fireplace."

Tyson walked across the room. The candle he had lit was still standing on the mantelpiece and he moved it from the left side to the right.

He had then looked along the leather-bound books to almost the last volumes.

He drew out the one he wanted but this time did not attempt to open it. Taking the candle from the mantelpiece he walked back to Vania.

As he reached her, he said:

"You realise, my darling, that it is you who has found my treasure for me?"

"It is what I . . . prayed I might do," Vania said, "but look . . . look quickly and see if your mother will help us as she has . . . helped us . . . already."

Tyson looked at Vania and knew that as far as he was concerned he had already found his greatest treasure, but he put down the candle and once again sat on the side of the bed.

He opened the small diary at the beginning and turned over the pages slowly.

"There is nothing in January," he said after a moment.

"February?"

"No."

Then at the last day of the month he stopped.

"Here it is!" he exclaimed.

"Tell me! Oh, tell me quickly!" Vania begged.

The writing was rather faint. Tyson bent

forward so that the light from the candle fell on the small book, and read:

"Hubert told me this Morning that He had an unmistakable 'Hunch' that there would be Trouble for the Southern County and Canterbury Bank.

" 'Why should You think That?' I asked.

" 'I have no Idea,' he said. 'I just Know it in My mind.'

" 'And what are You going to do about it?' I enquired.

" 'I think I will Drive into Canterbury,' he replied in a pre-occupied voice.

"I know when Hubert has One of His Hunches that it is Useless to argue with Him or try to Distract Him from doing what He wishes to Do. So I merely saw that He wrapped Himself up because it is very Cold today and He promised Me He would not be away Longer than He could Help. How I Hate the treacherous Winds at this Time of the Year."

"Go on!" Vania said as Tyson stopped speaking.

"That is all she writes for that day," he answered.

236

"But she must have said more . . . she must have!"

Tyson turned the page.

"Only about a fox killing one of the hens," he said. "Oh — yes!"

"What . . . does it . . . say?"

"Dearest Hubert has started a Cold since He came back from Canterbury yesterday Evening, so I cannot be Cross with Him for being Away so Long. He came into the House in a very Mysterious way, carrying an Enormous leather hold-all that I had Never seen Before.

" 'What have You there?' I asked, and he replied:

'It is Something I wish to take Up-stairs.'

"Briggs took it from Him and Hubert said:

" 'Put it in Madam's bedroom.'

"I thought then that He must have brought Me a Present and I was quite excited when He took Me by the Hand and We went up the stairs Together behind Briggs.

"Briggs put the Case down on the Floor of My room.

" 'Shall I unpack it, Sir,' he asked.

" 'No, thank You,' Hubert replied. 'We will see to it — and take a bottle of Wine to the Salon. I am Tired after such a long Day in Canterbury.'

"When Briggs had gone to My astonishment Hubert locked the Door.

" 'What have You brought Me?' I enquired.

" 'A fortune, My Precious Wife!' Hubert answered.

"I thought He was Joking, but when He opened the Bag I saw it was filled with Money — notes of £20 and £100 and also a lot of Gold Sovereigns.

" 'Hubert!' I exclaimed. 'Why have You brought all this Home?'

" 'Because I think it will be Safer with Me than it is in the Bank,' he answered.

" 'But where are You going to put it?' I questioned. 'It is Dangerous to keep so much Money in the House.'

" 'It will be quite Safe,' Hubert replied, 'because You and I, my Dearest, are going to Guard it Together.'

"I did not Know what He meant until He took off his Coat and to My astonishment started to take the cover off the Bed.

"It is so like Hubert to think of such a Strange, unusual Hiding-place that I just sat Down in a Chair and Laughed and Laughed."

There was silence as Tyson finished reading, then Vania asked:

"What did . . . she mean? I do not . . . understand."

Tyson stood up.

"I think I do," he said, "and quite frankly, it makes me want to laugh too."

"What does? Explain!" Vania said.

"Well, while we have been searching the house, looking behind books in the Library and making ourselves as dirty as a pair of chimney-sweeps, you, my precious, have been sleeping on enough money to keep us in comfort for the rest of our lives, even if I did not know I have inherited everything my grandfather owned."

Vania sat up in bed and looked at him wide-eyed.

"Do you mean . . . do you think . . . ?"

"I am just going to have a quick look," Tyson said. "Then we are going to sleep."

He moved to the end of the bed and pulled up the corner of the embroidered satin counterpane which covered the sheets.

Then he lifted first the top mattress made of soft goose-feathers, then the mattress beneath it, which was firmer and of lambs' wool.

Below, as the four-poster bed was very old, there was a third mattress sunk deep into a wooden box-frame that was carved and gilded on three sides.

The mattress fitted snugly into the box and it took all of Tyson's strength to prise up one corner and lift it.

By this time Vania had slipped out of bed and was standing beside him holding in her hand the lighted candle.

As Tyson turned up the cover of the third mattress, both their heads moved forward to look.

The candlelight revealed something that glittered and it was easy to see that besides all the shining coins there were packets of engraved bank notes.

"It is . . . there! It is . . . really there!" Vania said in an awed voice.

Tyson pressed the bottom mattress back into place and pulled the others down on top of it.

"It is where it has been for a large number of years," he said, "and it will certainly keep for the morrow. Get back into bed, my precious, and I will tell you how much it means to me."

Vania obeyed him and slipped between the soft linen sheets.

Tyson threw his robe on the chair, blew out both the candles and getting into bed, took her in his arms.

"Oh, darling, you have won!" Vania cried, turning towards him. "You have found the treasure! It is yours! Now we have nothing to worry about ever again."

"I have the only treasure which really counts here in my arms," Tyson said. "I knew tonight when you told me you loved me and proved it, my precious, beyond doubt that I was the most fortunate man in the whole world."

"Oh, Tyson, that is what I want you to think."

"It is not only what I think," he said, "but what I know, and, my perfect little wife, I shall spend the rest of my life convincing you that you matter to me more than anything else in the whole world."

"Now that you can prove you are Lord Wellingdale . . . Uncle Lionel will not . . . attempt to declare our marriage . . . illegal on the grounds that I am . . . under age," Vania said with a contented sigh.

"We will also know where our next meal is coming from, we can reward Briggs and Hawkins for their loyalty, and restore this house to its former glory."

"Oh, Tyson," Vania cried, "how wonderful it is that we can do all those things! I am so grateful, so very . . . grateful!"

"They are, all of them, unimportant

beside you, my lovely one," Tyson answered. "I love you so much that I can think of nothing else."

He kissed her as he spoke and, as she felt his hand touching her, Vania felt a little flicker of fire that once before had made her feel as if Tyson carried her into the heat of the sun.

It was there again, moving within her, making her body vibrate to his, making her hear the irresistible music of love enveloping her.

It was, she thought, like the songs of angels and she felt her soul join within, in a paean of gratitude because God had heard her prayers.

It was God who had saved her from marriage with Manfred Dale, from being kidnapped by Sir Neville and who had sent Tyson, like Perseus, to save her.

Perseus had married Andromeda and Tyson had married her. The fairy-story had come true and she must never forget to say Thank You.

"Thank You . . . thank you, God," she prayed, "and please show me how to make Tyson happy."

"I love you . . . Oh, Tyson . . . I love you!" she said aloud but breathlessly because his kisses were very passionate.

With a superhuman effort Tyson checked himself.

"I should let you sleep, my darling."

"How can we waste . . . anything so . . . wonderful as this . . . moment by . . . sleeping?" Vania cried. "I love you . . . Oh, Tyson, I love you and everything has come right for us both . . . I am your wife and we have found the treasure. But more exciting than anything else, you . . . love me!"

"You can be sure of that," Tyson said, "very, very sure, my precious one, as I will prove it to you over and over again for the rest of our lives."

His voice had deepened as he spoke. His lips, fierce, possessive and demanding sought hers again. The fire in them made the fire in Vania burst into flame.

Now he was carrying her into the sky and they were moving into the burning heat of the sun.

"I love . . . you . . . darling Tyson . . . I love . . . you."

"Give me yourself."

"I am . . . yours . . . all . . . yours . . ."

This was the treasure they had sought, the treasure of love that was more compelling, more irresistible, more valuable than anything else in the whole Universe.

About the Author

Barbara Cartland, who sadly died in May 2000 at the age of nearly ninety-nine, was the world's most famous romantic novelist. She wrote 723 books in her lifetime, with worldwide sales of over one billion copies and her books were translated into thirty-six different languages.

As well as romantic novels, she wrote historical biographies, six autobiographies, theatrical plays, books of advice on life, love, vitamins and cookery. She also found time to be a political speaker and television and radio personality.

She wrote her first book at the age of twenty-one and this was called *Jigsaw*. It became an immediate bestseller and sold 100,000 copies in hardback and was translated into six different languages. She wrote continuously throughout her life, writing bestsellers for an astonishing seventy-six years. Her books have always been immensely popular in the United States, where in 1976 her current books were at numbers one and two in the B. Dalton bestsellers list, a feat never achieved before or since by any author.

Barbara Cartland became a legend in her own lifetime and will be remembered for her wonderful romantic novels, so loved by her millions of readers throughout the world.

Her books will always be treasured for their moral message, her pure and innocent heroines, her good-looking and dashing heroes and above all her belief that the power of love is more important than anything else in everyone's life.

We hope you have enjoyed this Large Print book. Other Thorndike, Wheeler or Chivers Press Large Print books are available at your library or directly from the publishers.

For more information about current and upcoming titles, please call or write, without obligation, to:

Publisher
Thorndike Press
295 Kennedy Memorial Drive
Waterville, ME 04901
Tel. (800) 223-1244

Or visit our Web site at:
www.gale.com/thorndike
www.gale.com/wheeler

OR

Chivers Large Print
published by BBC Audiobooks Ltd
St James House, The Square
Lower Bristol Road
Bath BA2 3SB
England
Tel. +44(0) 800 136919
email: bbcaudiobooks@bbc.co.uk
www.bbcaudiobooks.co.uk

All our Large Print titles are designed for easy reading, and all our books are made to last.